The Tumbleweed Trail

Jake Preston, travelling with his wife and children, takes the Tumbleweed Trail, heading for Kansas City. And if the mile after mile of inhospitable terrain was not enough to contend with, there is the added complication of a gang of marauding bandits led by the notorious Sam Brady who have vowed to kill Jake and his entire family.

The family have only one hope and that is the mysterious stranger named Arkansas Smith, a man who some claim is an outlaw himself, a violator of women, a man as cold hearted as the bitter winds that often blow across the trail. But there are others who swear he is some sort of special lawman, a man bringing gun justice to those who need it.

There is only one certainty and that is that blood will flow along the Tumbleweed Trail.

The Tumbleweed Trail

Jack Martin

A Black Horse Western

ROBERT HALE

© Jack Martin 2019
First published in Great Britain 2019

ISBN 978-0-7198-2875-1

The Crowood Press
The Stable Block
Crowood Lane
Ramsbury
Marlborough
Wiltshire SN8 2HR

www.bhwesterns.com

Robert Hale is an imprint
of The Crowood Press

Typeset by
Derek Doyle & Associates, Shaw Heath
Printed and bound in Great Britain by
4Bind Ltd, Stevenage, SG1 2XT

This one is for my father and offered with the
greatest respect and affection

AUTHOR'S NOTE

The character Arkansas Smith first appeared in the 2010 novel Arkansas Smith, still available in print and eBook from Black Horse Westerns, and although this current work is a standalone story readers may also like to check out the earlier book.

From the diary of Ellie-May Preston

I fear the journey and I am convinced it is folly to travel as we intend; all our worldly goods packed in the small wagon Jake has purchased and travelling overland. It is a great distance to Kansas City and there are bound to be many dangers ahead of us. Dangers that we shall have no choice but face.

I have pleaded with Jake to change his mind. We have not much in the form of money but although I'm sure we can manage to raise the price of a train ticket for the family, Jake will not hear of it, he is as stubborn as a summer afternoon is fleeting. He says he wants to see the land again before it all vanishes and that it would be good for the children to undertake such a journey.

An education.

He claims it will be character building for them.

Honestly, sometimes I despair of Jake and his romantic view of the world but he is a strong man and I both love and respect him in equal measure. I have no choice but to trust in his judgement for there is no changing his mind. I pray to the Lord to give me the strength needed for such a journey. Life has been hard enough these last few years and I feel we are entitled some prosperity.

Once we had a good life in Wyoming and there was a time when we thought we would have remained working the farm for the rest of our days. And then when we had gone our bones would have been buried beneath the Wyoming soil and the children would have worked the farm, had children of their own and eventually handed the farm on to them. It would have gone on in that way for generations and there would have always been Preston blood working the farm and the bones of Prestons long gone nourishing the soil.

That was the way it should have been.

However after the war things had changed. Too many dry summers had withered the crops we grew and raped the goodness from the ground. And as the big corporations moved in and came to dominate the farming we found that a small farm such as ours could compete on neither price nor produce. The offer from Jake's brother to take up a new life in Kansas City is indeed a lifeline for the family.

Still I have this sense of foreboding deep within my soul and I fear the future we have ahead of us.

ONE

The night brought with it a cold wind and Jake Preston shivered as he pulled his coat tighter around his shoulders. He shifted closer to the fire and relit the stub of a cigarette that dangled between his dry lips.

'He's out there,' he said. 'Protecting us. There ain't nothing to worry about but worry itself.'

His wife reached over and gripped his arm, squeezing tightly and he suddenly felt warmth inside him. He looked at her and smiled, thinking how beautiful she was as the flames of the fire reflected in her eyes. Then he looked at his children, two girls and a fine young boy who would grow up into a decent man if this damn land would only let him.

'Time you young'uns was asleep. Come on, climb up into the wagon,' he said. 'We've got to start out at first light.'

There were several token groans but the children knew better than to disobey their father and one by one they kissed their mother and then sulked off to the wagon. It had been pitched at a safe distance from the fire but close enough that the dancing flames cast their tropical glow against the canvas and would offer reassurance to the children. It reminded them of the fire and they knew their parents were by the fire.

'What's that story?' Ellie-May asked, 'What kind of hogwash was that?'

'Ain't hogwash.'

'It is, too.'

'No it ain't,' Jake rubbed his eyes and smiled playfully at his wife. 'Tumbleweed's real enough. My pa told it to me and his pa told it to him before.' His eyes glazed over for a moment as he remembered the first time he had been told the tale. He had been little more than a babe in arms but it had stuck in his mind. 'And I expect his pa told it to him even before that.'

'And you believe it? You believe there's a man out there,' Ellie-May waved her hands at the almost pure blackness around them. 'You believe that there's a man out there who'd be,' she paused, working out the arithmetic. 'What, well over a couple of hundred years old? A man who protects folk travelling through these parts from any danger? From Indians? From outlaws? From the booger-man? A man who can change into a wolf, into any of the animals of the forest? You actually believe all that?'

Jake was angered for a moment but he shrugged his shoulders, figuring that it was Ellie-May's spirit that made her the woman she was. The woman he loved. He knew her questions were only half serious and that she was teasing him.

'There's no harm in believing it,' he said. 'It's real enough in here,' he added, pointing a finger to his heart.

Ellie-May looked at him with astonishment but then she grinned and reached across and kissed him on the cheek. She sidled over closer to him and hugged in beneath his arm. She stared at the flames and thought about the legend they called Tumbleweed. The tale may be hogwash but it was true that there was magic in the story and she did feel some comfort in believing that it was possible. That there could be some immortal man living in the wilderness, looking over the safety of weary travellers who journeyed along the trail that had been named for him.

'I love you, Jake Preston.'

'I love you too, Ellie May.'

'I'd better be climbing in with the children,' Ellie-May said after a short silence and when her husband nodded she broke their embrace. She groaned lightly as she stood, working a kink out of her back, and went off to the wagon, wishing her husband would come too but knowing he wouldn't. This wasn't Montana now, this was Colorado, Indian country and someone had to keep watch during the night. There were too many dangers for a family to be caught napping. And although there hadn't been any reports of Indian trouble for some considerable time there were many outlaws operating in the area.

She climbed into the back of the wagon and snuggled in between the girls. She looked over at Little Jake and smiled to find her son fast asleep in the corner, a thick woollen shawl draped over him. She was glad she had a husband like Jake Preston and didn't know what she would do without him. They still had some way to go before they reached Kansas City and it was comforting to know that Jake stood guard over them each and every night.

What need did she have of some mythical shape shifter when she had a real flesh and blood man to protect over her and the children?

Jake would never nod off, not even for a second. The little sleep he did get was taken during the day while she drove the four-horse team that pulled the wagon. She closed her eyes and felt herself drifting towards the inviting shroud of sleep but she would not dream of a fabled legend like the man called Tumbleweed, for there was only ever room for one man in her dreams.

And that man was currently sitting by the fire while he made himself another smoke from his makings. His brown papers were damp and he had to coax the cigarette to light but light it eventually did, and he sat there smoking and listening to the night.

He'd feel a damn sight easier when they'd gotten a few more miles beneath the wheels. They had set out from Wyoming and taken the old Bozeman Trail, travelling down through some pretty inhospitable country that had led them to Fort Laramie. There they had rested for a few days and replenished provisions before setting off again, initially following the Chisholm Trail.

Several days ago they had picked up on the ancient Tumbleweed Trail and Jake figured they were now somewhere around Pine Bluff, which was very much Cheyenne country. They would stick to this trail until they reached the Arkansas River and then follow the river towards Dodge City. It may have been a roundabout route but Jake figured under the current situation it was the safest way to go. From Dodge they would travel onto Ellsworth and then Abilene before picking up on the Chisholm Trail that would take them onto Kansas City and the new life that waited there.

It wasn't so much Indian trouble that Jake feared since relations between the whites and the Indians seemed to have eased somewhat in recent years, but one couldn't take anything for granted and there were still renegades out there. However, the threat that vexed his nerves the most was the possibility of an outlaw attack. There were outlaws hiding out all over this country and one man and his family would seem effortless prey to a bunch of owl-hoots in search of easy pickings.

There were terrible stories told of what outlaw bands did to women folk and it would be over his dead body before anyone laid hands upon Ellie-May or the children. Jake wasn't a killer, although he had killed during the war. Three men had died at his hands and each and every time he'd pulled that trigger, blasted those men because they wore a different coloured uniform, he had cried for the souls he had sent from the world. But if any man ever attempted to lay a finger of harm against his family, Jake knew that he would gladly send their blackened souls to Hell and shed nary a tear.

He finished his smoke and flicked the stub into the fire. Then he stood and worked the cold out of his legs before grabbing his Sharps rifle, the weapon he called Old Reliable, and taking a look around. He wouldn't go far though and would never stray further than shouting distance of the wagon.

It was said that the Cheyenne could make themselves sound like any animal they chose and Jake froze as he heard the lonesome call of a wolf from some far-off distance and wondered if the lupine howl came from a red man. He stood there, rifle gripped tightly, wide eyed and staring into nothing but blackness while the wolf, if indeed that was what it was, sounded again.

And again.

Feeling foolish, Jake shook his head. He smiled to himself, once more recalling the tale of the man called Tumbleweed. It was a legend he once believed but he had been a child then. Now he was a man and had no time for such fancies. Though, and he admitted it to himself, the legend was part of the reason he intended on sticking to the Tumbleweed Trail as much as was possible. If the legend wasn't true, which logically it couldn't be, then there was no harm in sticking to the trail, which would get them to where they were going as good as any other. And if indeed there did prove to be even the slightest grain of truth in the legends then it wouldn't hurt to have the added protection, supernatural or otherwise.

He was about to move further when he heard a sudden movement in the darkness. It came from ahead of him and not too away far. He pointed Old Reliable towards the sounds but could see nothing to aim at.

'Who is it?' he called and then in Mexican: 'Quien es? Quien es?'

There was no answer and Jake shook his head. He was getting jumpy and he scolded himself for his lack of courage. If he went around jumping at each and every sound he heard he'd twitch all the way to Kansas City. He shook his head again, muttered something beneath his breath and started back towards the wagon.

Whoosh!

There was no mistaking that sound and Jake knew an arrow had just flown over his head. He turned suddenly and fired off blindly into the night, then started running towards the wagon, screaming for Ellie-May to arm herself and prepare for a fight.

Jake didn't look back but kept running towards the wagon, concentrating on reaching his family and he ignored the blood-chilling screams that now filled the night air. They seemed to be coming from all around – to the left of them, the right of them, behind them and, Sweet Mother of Mercy – in front of them.

Jake screamed louder and broke out of the tree

cover. He could see the wagon in front of him. Ellie-May, her arms filled with the big old shotgun, was peering through the flap in the canvas. She saw her husband coming towards her and her eyes widened in terror.

Jake saw his wife raise her weapon towards him and he didn't have time to think about what was happening before the blast sent pellets whizzing over his head. He took a quick look back and saw the shadowy figure of a man, an Indian more likely, rolling about on the ground.

Whoever it was, Ellie-May had hit him.

'You darn nearly killed me,' Jake said.

He continued to run and he heard Indians in pursuit now. Terror filled his soul and he quickened his pace even more. He was almost at the wagon when he felt something underfoot as he kicked up a rock awkwardly. He couldn't keep his balance and he found himself pitching forward. He managed to hold onto the Sharps, but as he hit the ground he both heard, and felt, the bone in his left ankle snap.

'No,' he screamed, both in pain and frustration and rolled over onto his back. He let off three shots from the Sharps in quick succession and then heard Ellie-May jump from the wagon to come to his aid.

'Go back,' he screamed but the damn fool woman was true to her stubborn ways and she kept coming. She reached him and skidded to the ground on her knees. She grabbed him; eyes alert and placed a hand in the crook of his arm.

'Have you been hit?'

17

Jake shook his head. 'Broke my fool ankle,' he said just as two arrows thudded into the ground perilously close to their position. 'We've got to get to the wagon.' He fired the rifle again, the powder flash momentarily lighting up their surroundings.

Ellie-May glanced back at the wagon as if she were only then remembering her children. Little Jakie, God Bless him, all of nine years old, had armed himself with a rifle and was in the door flap of the wagon. He stared at his parents with both fear and immense courage in his eyes.

'Run, Pa,' he screamed.

'Come on, get me up,' Jake said and with his good leg pushed upwards at the same time as his wife lifted him. He placed Old Reliable in one hand and draped the other over Ellie-May. And with man leaning upon his wife they made for the wagon as quickly as they could. Little Jakie shot over their heads, aiming at nothing because he could see nothing but giving his parents some cover. The Comanche wouldn't be too eager to stick their heads up if there was a chance a stray bullet would take it off.

They reached the wagon and Jake leant against it while Ellie-May jumped up. Another arrow thudded into the side of the wagon and Jake tossed the rifle to Little Jakie and pulled himself up and through the doorway. Despite the pain in his ankle, he grabbed his rifle and stuck his head out, holding the weapon at the ready should he see a target.

He saw nothing, though.

Nothing, but a night as black as velvet.

Behind him the girls were crying and he could hear Ellie-May comforting them. Suddenly Little Jakie's head emerged through the canvas flaps and he smiled bravely at his father. He motioned to show he was still armed with the rifle.

Jake couldn't chide the boy and he felt an immense pride but that was quickly replaced by the most horrifying fear for his safety. He peered back out into the night but could see nothing and was greeted by a deathly silence. The Indians had ceased in their screaming and chanting. Jake wondered if they were at this very moment sneaking on silent feet, surrounding them. He had no idea how many were out there since he had yet to see a single brave other than the shadowy figure Ellie-May had shot.

Suddenly he heard gunfire in the distance and he recognized it for what it was – a rifle, but no bullet struck out anywhere near them.

Who was shooting?

And at what?

And then suddenly the night was once again filled with the roar of rifle fire and this was answered by further fire and the war cries of the Indians. It sounded like there was a full-scale battle going on but neither man nor boy could see anything, not a single powder flash.

'What's happening?' Ellie-May asked, her head suddenly appearing between the two Jakes.

'Someone's giving it to the Indians, I think,' Jake said.

'Who?' Ellie-May looked at her son and frowned when she saw the gun, looking impossible big in his hand.

'It's Tumbleweed,' Lucy said, her head appearing over her mother's left shoulder, the doll she called Miss Sally, dangling from a hand. 'Come to save us.'

There was hope in the young girl's voice and Jake would do nothing to contradict it, but all the same he told his wife to get her back inside. The shooting had stopped and Jake could hear the sound of horses receding into the distance while the yells of the Indians grew fainter and fainter. The Indians, still unseen, were retreating. Whoever it was out there they had saved their lives and he suddenly felt an immense gratitude for their saviours, whoever they were.

'Is it over, Pa?' Little Jakie asked.

Jake looked at his son and nodded.

'I think so, son,' he said. 'I think so.'

TWO

Jake didn't dare move and he lay there prone with the top half of his body poking through the wagon doorway, Sharps ready to be fired at the slightest hostile movement from the darkness. Inside the wagon Ellie-May bound his injured ankle with strips of material she had torn from an old dress. He had to grit his teeth against the pain. He'd taken nothing for it, not even a slug of whiskey; he'd never drink in front of the children, a rule that came from his own godly upbringing. Little Jakie maintained his position behind his father and he too lay on his stomach and stared into the silence of the night.

What the hell had happened out there?

Something like ten minutes had crawled by without any sound at all and so far nobody had approached the wagon. Jake didn't think it was a trick played by the Indians. He was sure they had gone but he had not the faintest inkling of who had come to their aid. Maybe it had been the legend called Tumbleweed, Jake thought and then smiled at his own foolishness. Tumbleweed was a trail-tale, a fairy story, nothing more. Something told to comfort children; an illogical impossibility designed by the human need for such fancies. Like the Tooth Fairy and Father Christmas, the man called Tumbleweed was not a man at all but a phantom of the imagination. It would be dawn soon and it couldn't come quick enough for Jake. As soon as it turned light enough to see where he was going, he would take a look around, broken ankle or no broken ankle. He'd take a chance.

He was suddenly reminded of that ankle when Ellie-May pulled a strip of the makeshift bandage a little too tightly but the pain, although intense, was momentary and left him even more alert. The woman had set the bone the best she could, and the splint and bandages had reduced the pain to a dull throb. Jake knew he wouldn't be able to walk upon it for some time but he'd be able to ride sure enough. Come first light he'd make some sort of crutch from the branch of a tree.

Whatever had happened out there, Jake planned on getting away from here as quickly as possible, and putting some miles behind them before the night fell again. And now his wife's head came back out between man and son and this time both of the girls followed. Five heads protruded from the doorway, all watching the sky begin to lighten slowly as dawn began to battle the night for dominion.

Jake tensed when he heard movement, like a twig snapping underfoot. He could see now, a few feet at least, and a milky almost ethereal mist floated just beyond the tree line, seeming to wisp in and around the trees.

He heard it again.

Someone was coming towards them.

'Who is it?' Jake called. 'Identify yourself. I'm armed.'

Lucy closed her eyes and mumbled: 'Tumbleweed.' She crossed her fingers and said it over and over again, as if wishing the man into existence. 'Tumbleweed, Tumbleweed, TumbleweedTumbleweedTumbleweed.' The word became one long verbal snake.

'Hello the camp,' came a man's voice and the man emerging from the opaqueness of the early morning could hear Jake's guarded sigh.

'If you're friendly,' Jake shouted back. 'You are most welcome. But if not I'll put a hole in your belly.'

Arkansas Smith suddenly appeared to them, as if magically materialising out of the mist. One moment there had been no one and the next he was there.

'Oh, I'm friendly enough,' he said and held his hand up as he approached the wagon. He looked at the five faces in turn and smiled. They were cute kids and the man and woman looked a handsome couple.

'I chased them critters that were bothering you off. You're safe now,' he said.

'Are you Tumbleweed?' Lucy, the youngest of the children, asked. She had her doll beneath one arm, clutching it to her chest.

23

Arkansas was taken aback by the young girl's question and he paused for a moment and then smiled. He too had heard the legends of the man called Tumbleweed, the benign spirit of the old trapper who supposedly protected the mortal souls of those who travelled the trail he himself had carved out of the wilderness.

'Stop bothering the man.' Ellie-May scolded her daughters and then ushered their heads back through the flap of the doorway. 'You are most welcome Mr, er—?'

'Arkansas Smith,' he said and dropped his arms. 'Ain't no Mr about it.'

Ellie-May and her husband exchanged a concerned glance, the name obviously meaning something to them, which didn't surprise Arkansas since his name was known across the West and even further afield. He took no pride in this but rather accepted it as a fact and a rather bothersome fact if truth were told. Everywhere he went it seemed some gunman out to make a name wanted to test their hand against Arkansas Smith. Those foolish enough to make a play usually ended up horizontal. Arkansas was tired of killing men that way.

'Then you are welcome, Mr Smith,' Jake said and finally put the Sharps aside.

'Arkansas will do. Anymore's a mouthful,' Arkansas said and removed his hat, shook the dust from it and then ran a hand through his thick hair before placing it back on his head.

The girls pushed back through the flap and this

time her mother ignored them.

'I'm Jake,' the man said. 'This here's my son Little Jakie, my wife's Ellie-May and those cute little bundles are Lucy and Sarah. We're all pleased to make your acquaintance, Arkansas.'

'Obliged to know you,' Arkansas said and leaned against the wagon. He looked directly into Jake's eyes. 'What you folk doing out here? Alone like this?'

'We're heading for Kansas City,' Jake said and then lowered his voice. 'Help me down,' he said. 'I've broke my fool ankle but all the same I'd rather talk away from the children.'

Arkansas nodded, held out his arms and grabbed Jake by the pit of his arms while he wriggled, serpent-like, from the wagon. Arkansas took his weight and Jake pointed towards the trees. Arkansas nodded and led the man a few feet from the wagon.

'Indians?' Jake asked.

'Sort of,' Arkansas said. 'A couple of rogue braves operating with a bunch of bandits. They like to make things look like Indian attacks to get the army all stirred up, chasing shadows while they plunder and kill. I've been following them for sometime.'

'You a lawman?'

Arkansas nodded. 'Something like that.'

Jake nodded, knowing that there was no use probing any further. He had heard the stories of the man called Arkansas Smith. Some said he was an outlaw, others claimed him a lawman and there were others still that said he was a combination of the two and so much more besides. Indeed if every story told about Arkansas Smith was given credence then the man would have been some sort of bizarre cross between Wild Bill, The Kid Antrim and Satan himself.

'You kill them?' Jake asked.

'I got one,' Arkansas said. 'A Texan known as El Asesino. And I think I winged another. And you folks got Running Elk.'

'We figured we'd hit someone,' Jake said. 'Weren't too sure, though.'

'You hit him sure enough. One of the rogue braves. I saw the body in the brush,' Arkansas said. 'Hit with a shotgun by the look of him. The others I chased away.'

'All on your lonesome?'

Arkansas smiled, weakly. 'They couldn't see me and they figured I could see them. I guess they didn't like those odds.'

Now it was Jake's turn to smile. He slapped Arkansas on the back. 'Let's hop on over to the wagon and get us something to eat,' he said with a smile. 'You hungry?'

'I could eat a horse,' Arkansas said. 'And speaking of horses I'd best get mine.'

Jake nodded and reached and snapped a branch from a tree before removing his arm from Arkansas's shoulder.

'You will eat with us?' Jake asked, leaning against a tree and cutting the branch into some sort of walking aid with his knife. He had the irrational fear that the man would vanish just as he had come.

Arkansas nodded and went back through the tree-line.

THREE

Arkansas crouched beside the body of the big Texan and shook his head.

'El Asesino,' he said. The name meant, *The killer.* 'I guess you won't be living up to that name any longer. The killer's been killed.'

Arkansas took a look around him and smiled grimly when he discovered a trail of blood that led into the thick foliage and then disappeared. So he had hit another one of them. He wasn't sure how bad he'd wounded the man but the fact that he had hit anyone at all was a miracle since he'd been firing blind, guessing positions, during a night so black it gave nothing away. With El Asesino dead and the brave the settlers had hit, it left seven members of the gang at large. And now they would know he was once again on their tail, that he had escaped the caves.

Brady's gang would be on their guard now. He cursed his luck. Why did the damn wagon have to pass this way and lull the gang out of their hiding hole? He had hoped to take the entire gang together, while they were off guard and he would have too, had Brady not decided to attack the wagon.

'Sure is a mess,' he said and spat a shred of tobacco out from between his teeth. He took another look at the big Texan and once more shook his head.

He supposed he had better bury the man. He may have been a bad man and never shown such courtesy to his many victims but Arkansas wouldn't leave anyone for the critters to gnaw on, not even a piece of trash like El Asesino. He'd bury the man; give him a better send off than he deserved and then do likewise for Running Elk, but not until he'd eaten.

He took one final look at the dead man and then went to his horse, grabbed the reins and led it through the trees towards where the wagon was parked. He whispered soothingly to the sorrel and patted the side of its head while he walked the magnificent looking creature, its coat showing a fiery red where the pale sunlight filtered through the trees, keeping in perfect step with its master.

'I sure hope you're still hungry,' Jake said as Arkansas emerged from the tree line and tethered the sorrel to a thick stump. 'Ellie-May's fried up some bacon, beans and a whole pot of coffee.'

Arkansas could smell the food cooking. The aroma immediately reminded him of how long it had been since he'd eaten anything other than a piece of cold jerky and he felt his stomach muscles tighten in anticipation.

'Hungry ain't the word for it,' he said.

Ellie-May emerged from behind the wagon. She had a pan in her hands containing a mess of steaming hot beans.

'You wash up,' she said and pointed to the stream. 'Just because we're in this wilderness don't mean we don't keep a clean table. Won't be a moment and I'll be dishing out.' She turned to the children and told them to get the plates from the back of the wagon and the girls did so while Little Jakie stood his ground, staring at Arkansas.

'Obliged,' Arkansas said and went to the stream, where he rolled up his shirtsleeves and splashed the freezing cold water onto his face. Feeling immediately fresh, he was just about to go get the food when he saw Jake come over to him. The man was limping. Without the use of his makeshift walking stick he would have fallen flat on his face.

'My girls are scared,' Jake said. 'Especially Lucy.'

'It's understandable.'

'Sure is.'

'I'm sure they'll be fine.'

'That's as maybe,' Jake scratched at his beard, as though figuring what to say next. 'Thing is, Lucy thinks you're this Tumbleweed.'

'The legendary Tumbleweed,' Arkansas smiled. 'It's a harmless enough tale.'

'You know the story?'

'Sure, don't everyone?'

'I guess so,' again Jake scratched at his beard. 'It gives her hope, I guess.'

'That's maybe the whole point of the story.'

'Is what I figure,' Jake scratched the beard so furiously that clumps of skin must have been coming up under his fingernails. 'Maybe she's better off believing it.'

'Figures,' Arkansas said and then laughed. 'And she thinks I'm this Tumbleweed!'

'She sure does.'

'You don't want me to tell her otherwise.' It wasn't a question.

'If you don't mind,' Jake said and smiled back. 'No harm in it. It'll make Lucy sleep easier to think Tumbleweed is watching over her.'

'No,' Arkansas said. 'I don't mind. I can think of worse things to pretend to be than some ghostly trapper turned guardian angel.'

Jake laughed again and slapped Arkansas on the back. 'Then let's be eating us a fill.'

'You'll get no arguments from me,' Arkansas said and allowed the man to lead him over to the fire.

From the diary of Ellie-May Preston

Jake is firm in his conviction that the move to Kansas City represents a new start for the family and ultimately a better life. He is resolute in this belief and whilst I have many concerns, I will not voice them, nor will I grumble, since it is the duty of every god-fearing wife to stand by her man. And Jake is a very good man and I will strive to be the best wife I can be.

We have been attacked during the night. At first we thought by Indians but we have since learned from a man who goes by the name of Arkansas Smith that it was an outlaw band with several rogue Indians among their numbers. The man, Arkansas Smith, saved us from certain peril but I have heard stories told of this man and if these stories are true then he is no better than the thieves and cutthroats that would have done us ill. He certainly looks like a gunfighter and wears his guns, two of them, tied down low as is the fashion with such people. However I must show charity towards him since without his intervention during the night we would have surely faced our doom.

Earlier Jake had been telling the children a bag of wind, that story of the mythical man known as Tumbleweed.

Honestly sometimes I swear he believes the tall tale himself. I intend to write the legend down within these pages when time allows but as far as I am concerned it's all fish stories and hot air.

It was during this attack that Jake stumbled and snapped his left ankle in two. I had to take up a weapon in our defence, as did Little Jakie, but we would sure have been doomed if not for this man Arkansas Smith.

The children all seem to have taken to him, Lucy especially who has convinced herself that the man is Tumbleweed himself. They say that children, unfettered by adult concerns, are able to read character far clearer than an adult, they can sense the good or evil in men. And whilst I do not know if I believe that, I do feel my children are no fools when it comes to judging people.

Jake too seems to trust the man and I know he hopes Arkansas will remain with us, ensuring our safety for the remainder of our journey.

Still, I am cautious of this man, and perhaps wise to be so. There have been deeds attributed to the man called Arkansas Smith that are too terrible to document, but by equal measure I have heard stories told of his great courage and sense of justice. For every one person who says Arkansas Smith is a scoundrel, thief and killer there are two more who swear him almost a saint.

I myself see none of this in his eyes. They are of the palest blue and seem guarded, hunted almost, like the eyes of a creature trapped in a snare. There is a kindness of sorts there, I can see that but the eyes are always alive, looking beyond the present as if preparing for dangers yet to come. He is very polite around me, courteous to a fault and acts like a gentleman of the finest breeding, but all the same I can sense him coiled like a spring and ready to go at any moment. Indeed if there is one feeling that Arkansas Smith gives off it is one of restlessness.

I must though be charitable and trust to the instincts of my husband and children. Jake is no fool and I do not believe it possible for him to be taken in by a charlatan and he is perfectly comfortable with this Arkansas Smith. I know Jake has heard many of the stories, both good and bad told of the man, but seems to have paid them no mind.

So I also shall not.

FOUR

'So you were trailing these men, why?' Jake asked. 'You already said you ain't exactly a lawman.'

Arkansas drew on the cigarette, feeling comfortable sitting besides the campfire with his belly full of the tastiest food he'd eaten for quite some time. Ellie-May and the children were down by the stream, washing the crockery while the men, Little Jakie included, sat by the fire. It seemed that Little Jakie, considering that he'd been there with gun in hand during the attack, had decided he was grown up enough to be eligible to sit around jawing with the men while the womenfolk carried out their chores.

Arkansas looked at the man for several moments before answering and he noticed that his silence was making the man nervous. He didn't want to do that, these seemed nice people and so he smiled and said: 'I've been trailing the gang for sometime. They've been hitting trains, wagons, stages and anything else that takes their fancy. They're not afraid to kill either.'

'But you ain't a lawman?'

'No.'

'Bounty hunter?'

'I work for the government,' Arkansas said and refused to be drawn further on the subject. After all what more could he say? That he had a death sentence hanging over his own head and that he was working towards a full pardon? That was more or less the truth, but it wasn't something he wanted to get into. Technically until that pardon came he was still an outlaw. He was doubtful that he'd ever get that pardon, and he guessed he'd be sent on one dirty task after another until he was killed himself. Or grew too old to be of further use.

Maybe they'd pardon him when he was an old man.

Maybe then and only then would the pardon be forthcoming.

Jake pulled a corncob pipe from his pocket and thumbed tobacco into the small bowl. He used a piece of kindling from the fire and sucked the tobacco to life, billowing pungent smoke from the corners of his mouth.

'You're after these men alone?' it was Little Jakie who asked the question.

'I do most things alone,' Arkansas said and smiled at the boy. The boy had the makings of a fine man and Arkansas could see from the pride in Jake senior's eyes that the man knew it.

'A man should always have someone else to share his troubles,' Jake said thoughtfully and stared deep into the fire. That sentence proved to be pretty much a conversation killer and for some time there was silence.

'I had a posse with me,' Arkansas said, presently. 'But Brady's gang ambushed us a ways back, killed some of the men and chased the others off. The posse are out there somewhere but maybe I'm the only one still trailing Brady's gang.' And with that explanation the conversation was firmly and finally laid to rest.

Afterwards Arkansas went to bury the two members of Brady's gang, with Jake insisting on helping. Little Jakie had wanted to come along but his father had made him stay with the wagon. 'Look out for the womenfolk,' he had told the disappointed boy.

The two men dragged the body of Running Elk through the woods, Jake wincing with the pain from his ankle but clenching his teeth and concentrating on the job at hand. They placed the Indian's body beside the big Texan and, working together, had a wide grave dug in no time. Then they hefted both men into the hole, figuring they'd rode together so they shouldn't mind eternity together, and tossed the dirt over them, finally patting down the mound with the back of the spades.

'You going to say a few words over them?' Jake asked, rubbing sweat from his brow with a rag from his pocket. He lowered himself to the ground and sat massaging his injured ankle.

'Wouldn't know how to,' Arkansas said and then

looked thoughtfully at the fresh grave. 'Guess them varmints' lucky enough we bothered to bury them.'

'Want me to speak for them?' Jake asked and hobbled to the head of the fresh grave.

'If it helps,' Arkansas said, though he wasn't sure any platitudes would help these two varmints into the hereafter.

Jake said his words, keeping it simple, mouthing the Lord's Prayer in a solemn tone and afterwards both he and Arkansas put an Amen to it.

They made their way back to the wagon, where Ellie-May had packed everything away and once again they were ready to move on. Little Jakie was sat up on the seat of the wagon, the rifle beside him while the two girls played in the stream.

'We're going to be striking off again,' Jake said and held out his hand to Arkansas.

Arkansas took the offered hand and they shook warmly. He thought for a moment of Brady's gang. There was no telling where they would be now that they had been flushed out of their hole. They'd lost two men in attacking the wagon and it would be unlike them not to try and get revenge further up the trail. Brady's lot were ruthless killers and they wouldn't spare the woman and children from their bloodlust.

'I guess I'll ride with you someways,' Arkansas said. 'Least till you reach Dodge. It'll be safe from there onto Kansas City.'

Jake smiled and slapped Arkansas on the back. He turned for a moment to wave to Ellie-May, signalling that he was coming and then turned back to

Arkansas.

'Pleased to have your company,' he said.

'Tumbleweed's coming,' Lucy said as she skipped past them and jumped up into the wagon. 'We'll sure be safe now.' The little girl was delighted with this turn of events.

Arkansas watched the little girl as she disappeared through the canvas doorway. Would they? Was anyone safe from Brady's cutthroats? He said nothing though and nodded to Jake, signalling for him to get up on the wagon.

'I'll ride up front some,' Arkansas said and went to his horse. 'Guess you should take drag.'

FIVE

The more Sam Brady thought about it the angrier he became.

He'd lost two men last night during what should have been easy pickings. And he himself had been winged, a slug creasing his left arm, but he'd bound the flesh wound and now that it had stopped bleeding, the pain had receded to a dull throb. He just hoped infection didn't set in and he was well aware that out here, without the attention of a doctor, even such a minor wound as this could prove fatal.

Someone had come up behind them, placed them in the crossfire between the newcomer and the wagon's people, and as unlikely as it seemed, the old bandit knew who that the newcomer must have been. It was that damn Arkansas Smith – somehow he knew that. Only Smith or an Indian could get that close to Brady without him being aware of it.

There was no other answer – Smith must have survived the caves.

'Damn the man,' Brady spat tobacco juice into the

fire. 'Why won't he just die?'

'Who?' Tommy looked up from the fire, his simpleton eyes reflecting the flames of the fire, his lips pursed as if still holding the question.

Brady got to his feet and walked over to a small tree at the edge of the clearing. He pulled his knife from its sheath and stabbed the flesh of the tree; over and over he delved the knife into the soft wood of the sapling, tearing away chunks as if it were his mortal enemy.

As if it were Arkansas Smith.

'Arkansas Smith,' he said and spun on his feet. His eyes blazing, he held the knife out before him as though challenging anyone who felt the urge to disagree.

'Smith's dead,' Tommy said and laughed but none of the other men joined in with the hilarity and all eyes were directed on the bandit who had led them for so long. Even the two Comanche stared at the old man with something like awe in their eyes.

'Is he?' Brady said with venom that silenced the laughter. Tommy may not have been the smartest of men; frankly he was a good throw behind an idiot, but he had learned enough about the old bandit called Brady to recognize the need for silence. 'Then like the Lord he's been resurrected.'

'Ressi-rec?' Tommy's face clouded over.

'Brung back to life, fool,' Jim Carter said and elbowed Tommy in the ribs.

'Brung back to life,' Brady mumbled and walked over to the Comanche known as Kicking Horse. The bandit knelt so that he was face to face with the Indian, who was lounging on the ground. 'You said there was no other way out of those caves.'

'There isn't.'

'Never trust an in'jun,' said the man known as Blade, on accounting of how he liked to skin people with the Bowie knife he carried, but everyone ignored him.

Brady pulled his Colt and stuck its ugly eye up against the Indian's forehead, which caused his companion Flightless Eagle, who was seated next to Kicking Horse to reach for his knife, but suddenly there were four guns pointed at him and the Indian held his hand clear of the weapon.

'Then how did Smith escape?' Brady asked and pushed the gun tighter against the Indian's head, leaving an indentation in the skin.

'Maybe he turned into a great bird,' the Indian said matter of factly. 'And flew out above through the walls of the cave.'

Brady stared at the Indian and he considered pulling the trigger, blowing his brains out, but that would be pointless. He holstered the weapon and stood up.

'Listen to me, you heathen fools,' Brady said, staring at the two Indians. 'Arkansas Smith can't turn into no damn bird. There must have been another way out.'

'He can turn into a bear,' Flightless Eagle said.

'What?' Brady knew these Comanche could talk considerable mumbo-jumbo but this was too much for the aged bandit.

'It is true,' Kicking Horse said. 'Many tales are told of the man the white-eyes call Arkansas Smith. The Comanche call him the Whispering-Wind. He appears out of nowhere and is a changeling. He can come as any of the creatures under the Great Spirit's sky. I saw him once turn into a bear.'

'You saw him?'

Kicking Horse nodded. 'I was but a boy and the man called Arkansas was surrounded by braves. He turned and fled into a great forest and then emerged as a bear. Eight of the ten braves died that day and the bear man escaped.'

'Why you fool,' Brady said. 'The bear must have already been in the forest. Men can't change into bears or any other animal.'

'No,' Kicking Horse was insistent. 'This was a man bear. I saw it.'

'Well I'll turn Arkansas Smith into a dead man,' Brady spat the words out and looked at the Indian with incredulity.

'The man called Arkansas Smith is bad medicine,' Flightless Eagle put in wisely.

'Well maybe he turned into a mole and burrowed his way out of them damn caves,' Brady said and stomped over to the fire. He knelt and poured coffee into a tin mug and ran a hand through his hair. He pulled his hat up from where it hung between his shoulder blades and plopped it back on his head.

'Heathen fools,' he muttered and spat tobacco juice into the fire.

The last few weeks had been a war and Brady felt like a weary general who had seen one too many battles.

He'd had a bad feeling about this from the get-go and although never one for caution, Brady wished that this time he had listened to his own intuition. That a posse had been sent out after them was no surprise. The last job had been an army payroll, and came after a string of bank and stage hold-ups, so it was to be expected. There was a large bounty on Brady's head and lesser amounts on the heads of each of his rapidly dwindling gang. At first the posse had been of little concern and Brady had merely kept ahead of them and waited for them to lose his trail, but the realization that the men were being led by Arkansas Smith had filled the bandit's heart with dread.

What was it they said about the man called Arkansas Smith?

That he walked like an ox, ran like a fox, swam like an eel and fought like a demon. He could spout like an earthquake, make love like a wild bull and swallow an Indian whole without choking. And what's more, according to the two Comanche fools he could change into any animal at will.

'Arkansas Smith,' Brady said without realizing he had spoken aloud. His men all looked at him but none said a word.

They'd first noticed the posse somewhere around Fort Laramie and had fled down towards Cheyenne but the posse kept pace, more than that it gained on them. Brady's gang had decided to lay in wait for the posse, ambush them. They had chosen a likely spot and positioned themselves in the rocks above a wide but shallow lake. The posse would need to cross the lake and the outlaw felt confident that he and his gang could wipe out most if not all of the men in the ambush. Once they had reached the lake there would be no cover for the posse and nowhere to run. The outlaws would be able to pick them off like targets in a shooting gallery. It should have been as easy as that.

And so Brady had spread his men out at strategic points in the rock face while they lay in wait for the posse, who could be seen as a faint dust cloud on the far horizon, to approach. While the bandits waited, Brady casually picked at his nails with the tip of his knife. He would look up from time to time, notice the posse had gotten that much closer, and then go back to the task at hand. Soon the posse were close enough for Brady to peer through his telescope and make out their faces. It was then that the bandit discovered Arkansas Smith was riding point, leading up the team of a dozen or so men. That had shocked the bandit. He had heard the rumours that Smith was now some sort of lawman but he hadn't believed it. And yet the sight he had seen through the lens confirmed it.

SIX

Jake moved his horse forward and then pulled up alongside Arkansas. He cast a glance over his shoulder at the wagon and then looked to the terrain up ahead. His injured ankle throbbed mightily but he ignored the pain.

'We're coming into some rough country,' he said.

Arkansas nodded but said nothing.

'Perfect place to lay an ambush,' Jake continued, and spat tobacco juice out of the corner of his mouth. 'Sure are a lot of places for a man to hide away.'

'Figured as much,' Arkansas answered without taking his eyes from the trail ahead. His face was without expression and there was coldness in his eyes. 'We'll keep on our guard.' It was only then that he turned to face Jake and when he spoke he smiled. 'I'd feel easier if you pulled back and rode drag. Protect the rear of the wagon.'

'Sure thing,' Jake nodded, turned his horse and galloped back to take up his position behind the wagon. He smiled at his wife and the girls as he passed them. Ellie-May was driving, the girls on the seat beside her while Little Jakie sat behind them, on the raised seat, cradling a rifle across his lap.

Overhead the sun was high in the sky, at its most powerful, and Arkansas figured they should stop to rest soon. They still had some ways to go and it was no use tiring out either themselves or the horses. Arkansas knew that Brady could attack them again at any moment, and when that happened he wanted the horses especially to have a reserve of strength should they have to outrun the murderous bandits. He and Jake could make a fight of it but he wanted to get the woman and children out of the way first. They were setting an easy pace but the afternoon heat was intense and made each and every step a major exertion. There was also the hint of a storm in the air, which added to the humidity and all in all made for some uncomfortable riding.

Arkansas noticed a bunch of cottonwoods ahead that would offer them some shade while they watered and fed the horses and took the time to rest themselves. They would also have a good view around them and if Brady did decide to attack they would see him coming. It was as good a place as any to rest up and when they pulled off again they would have to follow the trail through a valley and into the thick forest. It was then, Arkansas guessed, that the old bandit would take his chance and attack the wagon. He would still be smarting from the beating he had taken earlier and Arkansas knew Brady would be eager for revenge. The bandit was that kind of man and would feel driven to kill anyone who had crossed him. When he had attacked the wagon it had been with robbery on his mind, but the next time his guns would be answering a grudge.

Arkansas's orders, given over three weeks ago, were to hunt down and kill the old bandit. The powers that be had decided to save themselves the cost of a trial and wanted Brady shot down like the mad dog he was. It wasn't the kind of work that Arkansas relished but he had little choice in the matter, since he himself had a death sentence hanging over his head and was only at liberty in order to do the bidding of the government department led by Justice O'Keefe. Arkansas had been promised a pardon and as soon as it came he planned on riding away from this life, turning his back on O'Keefe and the lawmakers.

All Arkansas wanted was the sky above him, the ground below him and no barriers to his wanderings. He had been born a free man and he wanted that freedom back, for without it a man truly had nothing. There was no liberty in being a prisoner of circumstance.

Arkansas turned in the saddle and waved to Jake.

'We'll rest up yonder,' he shouted and Jake waved back in acknowledgement.

Only days ago Arkansas had had a posse with him. They had been a dozen strong but now half of those men were dead and the others had fled. He was all that was left and if that wasn't bad enough he now had a half crippled man, a woman and a bunch of children to concern him. Getting Brady should have been his chief concern but he had to get the Preston family to safety before he once again faced the old bandit.

Faced him for the final time.

His thoughts drifted back to the ambush Brady had laid for the posse maybe three days ago. Arkansas wasn't really sure, and he guessed it could even have been four days. He wasn't at all sure how long he'd stumbled about in the pure darkness of the cave system looking for a way out. But a way out he had eventually found and incredibly he'd discovered his horse close by, the well-trained sorrel drinking from a clear stream that ran down from the mountains while it awaited its master.

The ambush had been sudden and deadly and Arkansas still cursed himself for blindly leading the posse into it. Brady's gang had hidden themselves in the rocks and as soon as the posse rode into rifle range a deadly barrage had been let loose. Men had been shot from their horses; horses had been shot from beneath the men. Fire was returned but there was no clear target to shoot at and Arkansas had laid down low in the saddle and spurred his horse forward into a gallop, riding through the whirlwind of hot lead. He had reached the foot of the rock face but couldn't place any of the bandits to return fire. He dismounted, slapped his horse so that it ran off and hugged the rocks tightly, waiting for a chance to strike back at Brady and his murderous gang.

Arkansas had looked back at his own men and saw that they were being slaughtered; they were still returning fire when they could, but there was precious little for them to shoot at. The bandits were dug in well and able to use the rocks as cover so the fight was more a turkey shoot than a two-sided battle.

'Get back,' Arkansas had shouted to his men. 'Pull back out of range. They're murdering you.' He saw another member of the posse, Jim Jacobs, thrown backwards by the force of several bullets hitting him simultaneously. The man had danced about like a rag doll, seemingly suspended in thin air with his arms gyrating at his sides before his head exploded, sending a crimson blast into the air.

It was then that Arkansas noticed one of Brady's men on a ledge above him and he had shot quickly before the man could target any more of the posse in his sights.

The man had screamed and pitched forward into mid air, tumbling over and over in his fall, screaming until his lungs filled with air and burst. He was already dead before hitting the ground only feet from where Arkansas hugged the rock face.

Arkansas had begun to climb then, leaving his Winchester on the ground but keeping a Colt in his hand, the second holstered.

He spotted another of the bandits and fired, again hitting the man squarely and sending him falling to the hard ground below. The bandits had fired back but it was difficult for them to get a clear shot at Arkansas without revealing themselves and their slugs ricocheted with deadly music from the rock face.

Arkansas managed to reach a ledge and pull himself behind a large rock while bullets spat up chunks of rock and stone all around him. He reloaded his Colt and then placed a handful of cartridges on the ground beside him. If this was going to turn into a sustained fight then he was already at a disadvantage, one against many, six-guns against rifles. The one thing he had in his favour was his position, since he presented an impossible target, but soon Brady's men would grow bolder and several would move towards him while the others occupied his attention with blistering gunfire that would keep him pinned down.

Arkansas had crouched there behind the rock while he watched the remainder of his posse ride away into the distance. He had been left alone and in a perilous situation but there was nothing new in that and it seemed that his entire life had been one hazardous situation after another. True enough, he'd presented a difficult target for the bandits but he had nowhere else to go without allowing them a clean shot. Behind him the ledge ran along to a cave and Arkansas let off two wild shots, scooped up the unused cartridges, and then rolled towards it. Dust puffed up at his feet as several of the bandits changed position and were now able to shoot directly at him. He had gone into the cave, followed by a hail of gunfire.

He had hid himself in the darkness while he listened to the bandits approach the cave. He guessed he could maybe hold them off until the posse returned.

If the posse returned.

'Here seems as good a place as any,' Jake said, breaking Arkansas' reverie.

Arkansas felt himself torn back to the here and now and he looked at Jake. Ellie-May and the children were watching the two men, obviously eager to rest up themselves. They had gone many miles since first light and both the horses and people were feeling the strain of an increasingly humid afternoon.

Arkansas smiled – the threat of a coming storm felt stronger than ever, and resting up for a moment, replenishing their energies, seemed a good enough idea. If a storm did come then they would have to ride through it if they were to keep ahead of the bandits. Being fresh and dandy for it made perfect sense. There was also the fact that Jake, although uncomplaining, needed to rest up that ankle. He'd been in the saddle all day and his discomfort was evident in his eyes.

'Sure,' he nodded. 'Here's as good as anywhere.'

The diary of Ellie-May Preston

We have passed through some lovely country. I only wish we had time to stop and admire all the different wild flowers, the likes of which I have never seen. One particular flower, a dainty, fragile looking beauty with the palest red petals I have pressed into the back of this diary to identify later. Only yesterday we passed through a field of these flowers – they grew everywhere, their cheery faces poking out amongst the grasses and leaving off a sweet perfume as we went by. It is indeed a beautiful country but I have to keep reminding myself that it is also a dangerous country.

The man called Arkansas Smith has agreed to remain with us, at least until we reach Dodge. The country from there onto Kansas City will not be as wild and is better populated. There we will have the law to protect us from any bad men, whilst out here in the wilds the only law is that of the gun. There is however something about this man called Arkansas that troubles me, but all the same I am thankful he has agreed to ride with us. The protection he offers us is most welcome and although I know Jake would fight to the death to protect his family he has never really been a fighting man. He is a family man and I love him all the more for it. His strength comes from his dependability and his

53

sense of responsibility towards his kinfolk. To my mind this makes him stronger than any drunken brawler or flash gun-slick.

Lucy has particularly taken to Arkansas and she is convinced he is the fabled Tumbleweed. None of us have found it necessary to tell her otherwise, to destroy this childish belief. Jake says that if it gives her comfort then there is no harm in her believing. She is but a child and there will be plenty of time for her to discover fairy stories are not real when she grows up.

I have fixed Jake's ankle the best I can. All the while Jake gritted his teeth while his eyes rolled back in his head but he let out not a murmur, though I know he must have experienced intense pain. Lord, I swear as soon as we reach Kansas City I will never allow this family to wander again.

SEVEN

'We have to kill him,' Brady said. 'He'll keep coming until we do. We can't just ride away.' Brady knew that was true. If Arkansas Smith was after them then the only way to stop him was to face him head on. Smith would come and come until he was stopped stone dead.

Arkansas Smith was that kind of critter.

'Got to find the son-of-a-bitch first,' Jim Carter pointed out.

'My guess is he's with those folks from the wagon,' Brady concluded after a long moment, during which all eyes were trained upon the bandit leader. There was also the question of the remainder of the posse somewhere behind them, but Brady didn't really consider that too much of a danger.

No, the real threat lay in front of them.

'Yep,' Brady said. 'He's with that wagon, those sod-busters. And that makes him vulnerable.'

'How so?' Tommy asked, spooning the last of the beans from the pot.

Brady looked at Tommy and then shook his head at the man's constant stupidity. 'Getting us will no longer be his chief concern,' he said. 'He'll want to protect those sodbusters. We have to use that to our advantage or keep looking over our shoulders for the rest of our lives.'

'Won't be very long lives with Arkansas Smith chasing around after us. And if the rest of the posse return we could get stuck between them.' Blade spat tobacco juice onto the ground. He was a big man, aged somewhere around his mid-fifties, though no one knew for certain just how old he was. Rumour was he had ridden with both Quantrill and the James Gang at one time or other, but no one could say if that was true or not. What was certain was that for the past couple of years he had been a part of the Samuel Brady outfit. Blade was a cold-blooded killer whom, as another legend had it, had killed his own ma for the few dollars savings the old woman had hidden away in an Arbuckle's coffee tin.

'Then what are we waiting for?' Jim Carter asked. 'He took us by surprise last night but it won't happen again. Let's ride down upon them now. Now's a good a time as any for a killing.' He pointed his Colt at thin air and mimed shooting. Then he smiled, kissed the butt of the gun and returned it to its holster.

'I'm all for that,' Blade said and smiled. His teeth were like gravestones in the slit of his cruel mouth.

Brady looked thoughtfully at his men and then shook his head. The wind was picking up and he pulled his collars tighter around his neck. Briefly he cast his eyes at the far horizon, at the darkening sky. Brady was a superstitious man, always had been, and he wondered if the muddy sky was some kind of omen.

'Before this is over Arkansas Smith will be dead,' Brady said with a firm conviction that he just didn't feel. 'But we ain't just attacking blindly. We need to be smart. Smarter than we were with those so-called inescapable caves,' Brady aimed the last remark at Flightless Eagle but the Indian's expression remained impassive.

The failure to kill Smith in the caves still rankled with the bandit. The man should have been a sitting target, and Brady had been about to send a couple of men in after him when Flightless Eagle had pointed out that there was no other way out of the caves. With them standing there at the cave mouth it meant that Arkansas was trapped, his one avenue of escape blocked by their guns, and so they had lit a huge fire in the cave mouth, dragging a mass of kindling and dead bushes onto the flames, sending billows of suffocating smoke into the caves.

Then, with the last of their dynamite, they had caused a landslide cutting off what, they had believed, was the one and only exit. If the smoke didn't choke Arkansas to death then he would eventually succumb to starvation. It was the latter option that appealed to Brady since it meant the man would suffer all the more. The thought of Arkansas Smith driven half mad by starvation, stumbling about in the darkness until he finally fell down dead, had been a good one.

Only Flightless Eagle had been wrong.

There must have been another way out.

'Flightless Eagle,' Brady said. 'I want you to ride on ahead, find out where Smith and the sodbusters are at this present moment and then come back and let us know. We'll be following behind at a steady pace, keepin' the horses fresh for the attack. This time we're gonna send them all to hell and there won't be no mistakes.'

The Comanche nodded, said nothing and immediately went for his horse. He mounted up and, pausing for only a moment to look at Kicking Horse, he sent the horse galloping.

Within moments he had vanished from view.

'Kicking Horse,' Brady said. 'You go in the other direction and find out how far back that posse is. The rest of you mount up and let's ride.'

The men set about collecting their belongings together and saddling their horses. Brady stood beside the fire, watching them. His gang now totalled but six men including himself, but the old bandit knew that was more than enough to do the job at hand. If Smith hadn't taken them by surprise that night, if they'd known he was there, it would have been a different story. Had that been the case then Brady had no doubt that both Smith and the sodbusters would now be dead.

As soon as the men were ready Brady poured the last of the coffee over the fire and then kicked dust over the hissing embers. He walked over to his own horse, which was already saddled, and pulled the Sharps Big Fifty from its boot. He was an expert with the powerful weapon, capable of hitting a five-inch bullseye at more than 200 yards. The weapon took massive three and a quarter inch cartridges and was not for nothing known as the Buffalo Gun. When it hit it was with devastating force and during the war Brady had seen men torn apart by the weapon. It was intended to be shot from a rest rather than the shoulder but Brady was a bulky man and by adapting the stock and carving into the butt he had no problem using the gun as if it were a much smaller weapon. He could even shoot it while mounted but his accuracy was somewhat reduced. He went through the usual checks on the weapon and then replaced it in the boot.

He mounted his horse.

'Let's ride,' he yelled and spurred his horse, all the while thinking of Arkansas Smith trapped in the sights of that big old Sharps.

EIGHT

'Coffee's mighty tasty,' Arkansas said and watched as Ellie-May removed the straps from her husband's injured ankle. The ankle was swollen and the bruising had turned the entire foot an ugly purple colour. If the ankle didn't set correctly then the man would forever walk with a pronounced limp, and if infection set in there was a chance he'd lose the whole darn foot from the ankle down.

Jake forced a smile but the beads of sweat being squeezed out of his forehead revealed the intense pain he was feeling. He winced slightly as his wife gripped the ankle and started to massage it slowly, feeling for the broken bone.

'I've done the best I can,' Ellie-May said. 'But I think you need a sawbones to look at this.'

'Want me to take a look?' Arkansas asked.

'You know how to set a broken bone?' Ellie-May asked.

'Some,' Arkansas said and knelt over Jake. 'I had cause to help a few men out during the war.'

Ellie-May nodded and moved aside.

'Obliged to you,' Jake said.

Arkansas gently gripped the man's ankle and then moved his hands up and down across the joint. He could feel the break and he figured it was clean and would mend nicely given the chance. In a perfect world Jake would be able to take to his bed, rest up for a few weeks and then be as good as new. As it was, with the arduous journey still ahead of them he guessed the man would recover sure enough but would most likely hold a reminder of the injury in his step forever.

'If you were a horse,' Arkansas said with a smile. 'I'd recommend shooting you but as it is I think you'll be fine. I'll need to pop this back into place.'

Jake nodded, gritting his teeth against the discomfort. Even with Arkansas handling the ankle gently as if it were a new-born kitten there was still pain; considerable pain.

'You may want to slug some whiskey,' Arkansas suggested. 'I've got a little in my saddle-bags.'

'No,' Jake shook his head. 'Just do what has to be done.'

'Please be careful,' Ellie-May chipped in and then turned away and went to sit with the girls, who were playing in the dirt at the front of the wagon. Little Jakie stood off to one side, cradling the rifle.

Arkansas felt for the break and then gripped the ankle tighter. 'This is going to hurt some,' he said.

'Just do it,' Jake said, grit in his voice. And then whined. 'Quickly.'

'I'm about to.'

'Then do it. The quicker the better.'

Arkansas suddenly twisted the ankle. The pain must have been intense as he twisted some more until he felt the bone snap into place. The break came together with a clicking sound, but Jake uttered nary a groan and sat there with his teeth grinding together. Arkansas then gripped the ankle tighter still, squeezing, else that bone snap apart again and called for Ellie-May to reapply the bandages and splint, telling her to bind the ankle as tightly as possible but not cut off the blood flow.

The woman didn't need telling twice and she ran to his aid.

'Is that it?' Jake asked, presently. His face was so wet with sweat that he looked as if he'd just bathed. He didn't quite smell as fragrant, though.

'That's it,' Arkansas nodded and smiled grimly when Jake fell into blessed unconsciousness. 'Best bind the ankle tightly now while he's out. Less pain that way.'

Ellie-May nodded and looked with concerned eyes at her husband, thinking how peaceful he looked, as if he had fallen into a restful sleep. She expertly applied the bandages, pulling them tightly and knotting them around the foot.

'Best leave his boot off,' Arkansas said. 'He'll need to keep his weight off the foot so he won't need the boot. It'll be more comfortable for him without.'

'I'll put an extra layer of bandage around the foot,' Ellie-May tore a long strand of material from her shawl. 'One thing I got plenty of is clothes,' she said. 'Most of them are rags though.'

'Needs must,' Arkansas said.

'When we get to Kansas City,' Ellie-May said without looking up from the task in hand, 'I'm going to buy myself the sweetest dress you ever did see. And the children too. I'm going to kit them out with new clothes and wash all this trail dust away. We sure enough deserve it. After all this we sure enough deserve it.'

Afterwards, Arkansas stood besides the small campfire, smoking a quirly and sipping the last of the coffee. Jake, now conscious, sat beside him, the injured ankle resting on a rounded rock.

'We need to be moving on,' Arkansas said. 'There's a storm brewing and we've still got some mighty rough country to cross.'

'I'm ready,' Jake said and lifted himself to his feet. The new crutch that Arkansas had carved from the sturdy branch of an Alder made getting about easier and now that the break had been set, Jake found the pain much more bearable. He could hobble about with the crutch pretty much unaided.

Arkansas smiled as Lucy ran behind them, being chased by her sister, who held a long worm dangling from her fingers. He watched them for a moment, enjoying the childishness of their game, and as Sarah caught up with her younger sister and dropped the worm down her back, he laughed. Lucy screamed in disgust and fell to the floor, arching her shoulders, kicking her legs, and yelling for someone to 'get it out, oh please get it out. It's 'gusting!'

The screams were the cue for Ellie-May to get involved and she scolded Sarah, before lifting Lucy and shaking the worm out of her clothing. The creature fell to the dirt and, seemingly unfazed by its ordeal, slithered into the ground.

'Get into the wagon, girls,' she said and then looked at Arkansas and her husband. 'Guess we're ready to move on.'

Little Jakie emerged from behind the wagon, still holding the rifle and saying nary a word, he climbed up onto the wagon and sat himself down in the seat. The boy had already checked the team that pulled the wagon and had, in fact, kept pretty much busy throughout their stop. As soon as he had eaten he had gone and fed and watered the horses, as well as the pack mule, which ambled along behind the wagon. The boy was quiet and Arkansas recognized the look of intense concentration in his eyes. Now that his father was injured the boy felt that he had taken on the role of protector to the womenfolk. He'd grow up into a fine man one day, Arkansas thought. As fine a man as his pa seemed to be.

Arkansas helped Jake cross to his horse and lifted the man, making a stirrup out of his hands and pushing while Jack swung his bad leg up and over the saddle. He then guided the man's injured leg into its stirrup and made his way to his own horse, knowing that Jake would have been better riding in the wagon but the man wouldn't hear of it and wanted to be in

the saddle, looking out for his family as they continued on their journey.

'I'll continue riding point,' Arkansas shouted back
over his shoulder. 'I'd like to reach the Great Forest
as soon as we can. There's a storm brewing and the
forest trail will mean we're less exposed. You take up
the drag.'

Jake said nothing and it was clear from the set of
his mouth that he was experiencing considerable
pain after getting up into the saddle. He immediately
turned his horse and took up position at the rear of
the wagon.

'Let's kick up some dust,' Arkansas yelled and
gently spurred his horse into motion as the sky above
them turned a foreboding cobalt blue.

NINE

Flightless Eagle whispered soothingly to his horse while he watched the wagon making its way through the long grasses that stretched for many miles towards the valley. From his vantage point he could see Arkansas Smith clearly heading up the trail. The Indian mumbled an ancient prayer to ward off the bad medicine that surrounded the man he thought of as Whispering Wind.

There were only the two men – Smith riding up front and the sodbuster bringing up the drag. Flightless Eagle wasn't sure how many people were in the wagon but he guessed it would be the sodbuster's woman and the children. He was sure that as soon as Brady learned all this, the old bandit would want to attack at once. He would like these odds and would prefer to kill off Arkansas Smith and the sodbusters before the surviving members of the posse returned and strengthened their numbers. Two men and a woman and children would be no match for the outlaws but all the same Flightless Eagle felt uneasy.

There was no honour in slaughtering women and children.

He remained where he was for many minutes, watching the wagon until it had entered the thicket and vanished from view. The trail snaked its way through the tall grasses that could cover a man in places. Miles distant was the valley and beyond that still the massive forest, through which the trail went for many miles before emerging into the hills that stretched onwards to the Arkansas River. It would take two days for the wagon to travel through the forest and it would be easier to sneak up on the sod-busters before they emerged into the hills. With the cover the numerous Whitebark and Ponderosa pines provided, the Indian was sure they would be able to get close enough to the wagon to pick the men off before they even knew what had hit them. This was not the way the brave liked to fight, there was no honour in facing an enemy unless it was face to face, but then he knew that Whispering Wind was no mortal enemy and perhaps the only way to strike the man down was by swift surprise, not allow him the chance to react and bring his bad medicine into practice.

Flightless Eagle turned his horse and kicked it into a gallop, back towards Brady and the men.

TEN

Arkansas cursed.

They had been making good time and had already entered the valley but he would have preferred to cover another couple of miles before nightfall, maybe even make the outskirts of the forest. However, they had been forced to stop because the wagon had thrown a wheel.

'Maybe we'd better make camp here,' Arkansas said, examining the wagon. The wheel could be repaired but it would take a little time and darkness was not that far off.

Jake nodded, knowing that with his injury he would be next to useless in helping to repair the wagon. It looked as if the low humidity and high temperatures had caused the sleeve that held the wheel on its axle to shrink and split. A new sleeve would have to be carved and then the wheel reattached and coated in grease and tallow. The wheel itself looked fine but the axle had split and caused the wagon to tip onto its side.

'We'll have to find something to lever the wagon up while I repair the axle,' Arkansas said and looked around. There were a few scattered trees here and there and he was sure he'd be able to find something suitable among them. 'Guess I'd better find a strong enough branch and get chopping.'

'Obliged,' Jake said and slid from his horse. He leaned against the beast, keeping his injured foot off the ground while he slid his crutch from the straps that held it to his saddle. 'There's an axe in the tool box on the wagon.' He turned to look at his son. 'Go get it boy.'

'I'll fix a fire,' Ellie-May said. 'Get some coffee brewing.' The girls, seeing this as another chance to run around, work the cramps from their young legs, bounded past her.

'Don't go out of sight, girls,' Jake said. 'It's all too easy to get lost in this thicket. You don't want to get gobbled up by a bear now.'

Little Jakie jumped from the wagon, axe in hand and took it over to Arkansas.

'I can help you,' the boy said.

Arkansas took the axe from the boy and then nodded. 'Come on then,' he said. 'Let's find us a suitable lever.'

Jake watched his son follow the man called Arkansas into the thicket and remained watching until they had vanished from view. He looked up at a sky already darkening with the coming of night. There was a certain freshness about the air as if in anticipation of the coming storm and Jake felt that the storm might be closer than they had previously imagined. If the rain, when it did come, was heavy and sustained for any length of time, it would turn the trail into a mud bath, making their already difficult progress more arduous still.

As Jake stood there, using the crutch for support, watching Ellie-May fix a fire while the girls, Lucy holding onto the ever-present rag doll she called Miss Sally, ran about being chased by her sister. Not for the first time, Jake doubted the wisdom of leaving Wyoming in the first place.

True they had done well enough thus far – with the light wagon and the small team pulling they had been able to cover ten to fifteen miles a day, keeping up a mostly constant speed of around two miles an hour. And until the bandit attack the journey had been largely uneventful. They had run into Indians at Lusk but they, a wandering bunch from the Blackfoot tribe, had been friendly enough, even trading one or two items with Jake and his family. The buffalo hides that kept the girls warm as they slept had come courtesy of the Indians and cost only two imitation pearls and a leather canteen. It made Jake feel like a cheat but the Indians had been pleased enough with the smooth balls that he had snapped off Ellie-May's neck chain.

Leaving Wyoming though, had been the correct thing to do and Jake knew that. Deep down he knew that. There was not a single tangible doubt in his mind, least not one that lasted, and the anxieties he felt on occasion were, he supposed, only natural.

The farm he and Ellie-May had built up from nothing was failing and had no hopes of competing with the big corporations who were now farming what little land was left available. They'd made a living but nothing more and were able to feed and clothe themselves but never able to indulge in even the most meagre of luxuries.

Working the farm was a constant battle against the elements; days spent in the fields from dawn to dusk for precious little reward. And what crops they did produce were then sold to the market at too low a price in order to compete in an increasingly aggressive environment. The grasshopper invasion a few seasons ago had all but finished them off and Jake still shuddered when he recalled the sight of the untold millions of grasshoppers, a column of the things a hundred and fifty miles wide and almost that in length. There had been so many of them in that pulsating storm that they had turned day into night. Those critters had eaten crops across territories. Damn near chewed their way across the entire West and folk still called it The Great Grasshopper Year. It was a year that Jake's farm had never really recovered from.

The offer to take up a position in Kansas City couldn't have come at a better time. Jake felt it offered the entire family a future that was beyond their grasp in Wyoming. It had been Jake's brother, William, who had made the offer for Jake to work for the thriving Preston Cattle Company.

William had initially made his money trading

along the Missouri River before becoming involved in the cattle trade. And after making a handsome profit on his first outfit, the entrepreneurial William Preston invested in a bigger herd and never looked back. The Civil War had been good to William and he had secured an army contract that allowed his organisation to grow and continue to do so after the fighting ended. William, by now wealthy, had then become an important figure and his involvement in politics seemed a natural step for him. When the Missouri Pacific Railroad reached Kansas, William had been in a perfect position to ensure his own business interests benefited from the influx of activity that the railroads brought and would continue to bring. These days Kansas City was one of the busiest train centres in the entire United States. It was all a far cry from Jake's own farm that seemed to produce nothing but blood, dirt and blisters.

William's offer had been a lifeline to Jake and had not taken much thinking over. It was a good offer; a generous offer and not one Jake could afford to turn down. After all, as it had said in William's letter – *These days my political duties occupy the bulk of what little time I seem to have and I am neglecting my business interests. I need someone I can trust at the top, as there are many who would conspire against me and line their own pockets disproportionately to their labours on my behalf. Who better to trust than one who shares blood? Should you accept the position, my dear brother, I am sure it will be of mutual benefit.*

Jake had accepted the offer but insisted on

making his way to Kansas overland and under his own steam. His brother had offered to pay the train freight but Jake wouldn't hear of it. One offer was generous enough, but he certainly wasn't going to accept charity. He may not have much in the way of material possessions, but he had his pride and whatever rewards he found in Kansas would come from his own hard work, even if it was on his brother's behalf. And besides, Jake had told Ellie-May, it would be nice to see what was left of the country before it was all gobbled up by progress. He spat the word progress as if it were dirty, and perhaps, to Jake's way of thinking, it was.

ELEVEN

Brady grinned and ran a hand across his mouth. There was juice from the beans he'd just eaten encrusted in his beard and he scraped this away with his fingers. 'Land of many trees,' he said, smiling at Flightless Eagle, crusty dandruff falling from his beard and floating on the air like blood-soaked snow. 'You mean the Great Forest?'

Flightless Eagle nodded. 'The land of many trees. One more sun and they shall be there.'

'Heathen,' Brady muttered and stood eye to eye with the Indian. It made the outlaw a little uneasy that the brave didn't flinch in the slightest, but he smiled and slapped Flightless Eagle on the back.

'You did well, red man.'

'The Land of many trees,' Flightless Eagle repeated, impassively. 'One more sun.'

Brady paced for a moment, lost in thought. From what Flightless Eagle had told him, Brady figured it would be easy to ride out ahead of the wagon and conceal his men amongst the trees, spread out and then ambush the wagon as it approached the forest. Neither the sodbusters nor Arkansas Smith would have any chance since there was only the one trail through the forest that could accommodate a wagon and Brady and his men would be spoilt for choice as to concealing themselves.

This time the ambush would work – earlier when Brady and his men had ambushed the posse along the cliff face there had been too many variables, too many places to run and the posse only had the one frontal attack to face, but this time Brady would be able to surround the wagon and pick them all off one by one, the children too would perish under the merciless hail of lead Brady and his men would send their way. The bandit intended on leaving no witnesses to the attack and he knew they would all have to die, no matter how young.

He himself had already lost too many men and he wasn't going to take any more risks.

Arkansas Smith and those that travelled with him would have to pay a high price for getting in his way. The bandit didn't particularly relish the thought of gunning down women and children but he had no other option. He didn't intend on running forever and he would do what he had to do in order to keep his liberty. If he killed the men and allowed the women and children to continue on their way they would eventually tell their story and then even more posses would ride out after The Brady Gang.

Brady was tired of the constant chase.

'Mount up,' Brady ordered. 'We've no time to

waste. Let's get this over and done with.' Kicking Horse had not yet returned, which Brady figured meant that the remainder of the posse were many miles back.

'It's about time,' Jim Carter said. 'I'm getting mighty tired of all this hiding away. Ain't no profit in it.'

'All things will come,' Brady said and spurred his horse forward, taking up the lead, while his men followed behind. Though in truth the bandit didn't feel much like a leader and all he wanted was to disappear somewhere and rest up for a month or so without anyone looking to him for guidance. He was bone weary and was starting to feel his age. In his profession reaching old age was a rarity but he could feel it coming on him.

As soon as Arkansas and the sodbusters were dealt with Brady planned on splitting up the gang, going his own way, finding somewhere peaceful to live and changing his name, his appearance. For longer than he cared to remember he had worn the thick facial hair and he guessed he'd look like a different man without it. All it would take to transform Sam Brady into an anonymous nobody was a sharp razor and some hot water.

The country was changing, the old bandit may not have had any schooling but he was smart enough to realize that the end was coming for him and his kind. Civilization was approaching on even the most remote country and with it came the politicians and their laws, and then would come the sheriffs, the marshals, the lynch-happy posses, and one by one the old outlaws would be run into the ground and hung under the name of a vengeful law.

There was a time when a man could ride for days, weeks, even months, without any trace of another living soul but all that was changing. These days the railroads criss-crossed the country, swallowing and mutilating once virgin ground and destroying habitats of critters that had been there before men had even set foot in the country. The trains simply moved along, chug-chug-chugging a song of despair as they went by. A few months ago Brady had been in California and he'd watched the railroads bringing the endless trains into the once gold-rich country. He imagined that one day there would be no land left, every inch of ground from ocean to ocean covered in the dull coloured rails that carried the iron monsters and it wasn't a prospect he relished. The endless trains would spew their black smog into a once clear blue sky and choke all those that lived beneath it, smother them in the thick cloud of civilization.

'What's the plan?' The speaker was Blade. He had galloped up to Brady. The man skilfully slowed his horse to a trot that perfectly matched Brady's pace.

'Kill them all,' Brady said without looking up from the trail ahead.

'All of them?'

'All of them.'

'Women and kids too?'

'All of them.' Brady insisted.

'Men might want to have some fun with the

woman,' Blade said with a tight grin. 'That is before putting a bullet through her head.'

Then Brady did turn to face the man and there was a look on his face that silenced the other man.

'No one touches the woman,' the bandit leader snarled. 'They all die but they die quickly and cleanly, none will be molested. We are men, not animals.'

TWELVE

'Get some more grease on that axle,' Jake said, his injured ankle meant that he was beyond offering true aid with the repair to the wagon, but he made himself useful by supervising. Well he considered his input useful but to Little Jakie and Arkansas, who laboured in refitting the wheel, he was a hindrance, although neither of them said so.

Arkansas dug his hands into the tin of animal fat and smeared it liberally along the axle, taking particular care to cover the newly constructed sleeve that held the wheel in place. The grease would help protect the wood from the elements and as long as fresh grease was applied regularly, Arkansas felt the wagon could make the rest of the journey without further mishap.

'Stand back, boy,' Arkansas pushed Little Jakie back slightly while he gripped the pole they had used to lever the wagon up so that they could make the repair. The fifteen-foot-long pole was placed securely beneath the wagon with the other end resting on a large rock and then tied down to the ground with strong rope to create a kind of seesaw, which lifted the wagon just high enough to give clearance to carry out the repair.

'Be careful there,' Jake said and hobbled over to Arkansas. He gripped the end of the pole and winced when he felt a stab of pain in his ankle, but he ignored it. The wagon had to be lowered down gently to prevent further breakage. If the wagon was dropped too forcefully to the ground the axle could snap in two.

Arkansas pushed his weight down onto the pole and looked Jake straight in the eyes. 'You ready to take its weight?' he asked.

Jake nodded, gritting his teeth.

'OK, boy,' Arkansas said and turned to Little Jakie. 'Release the securing ropes.'

Ellie-May and the girls came from the campfire to see if they could be of help but Jake ordered them to stand back, adding a command to his wife to get some more of that delicious coffee ready.

'Foods gonna' taste mighty good after our toil,' he hinted with a tight grin.

Afterwards they all sat around the campfire, their bellies full, their bodies relaxed. The threatened storm had held off and it was a mild evening but Arkansas didn't think it would remain this way for too long. He could smell the distant rain in the air and he knew it would come, a lifetime spent outdoors told him so. By dusk tomorrow they should reach the Great Forest and if the storm held off until then it shouldn't hinder them too badly, but riding across the valley towards the forest would be a nightmare with a storm blowing in their faces.

'Come on, girls,' Ellie-May said, clapping her hands. 'You two need your sleep.'

Lucy and Sarah's faces dropped somewhat but they never said a word and promptly stood up, kissed both their mother and father, and then smiled at Arkansas and Little Jakie. Lucy then stepped closer to Arkansas and bent and pressed Miss Sally's face against Arkansas's, as if the doll was kissing the man.

'Miss Sally like you,' she said and then followed her older sister to the wagon. They climbed up into the box and Ellie-May went after them to settle them down for the night.

'You've got a fine family,' Arkansas said, smiling at Jake and rubbing the side of his face as if the doll's kiss had left moisture upon his skin.

'I sure think so,' Jake said and with a groan bent to the fire and pulled out a twig, which he used to light a quirly. He tossed his makings to Arkansas.

Arkansas quickly made himself a smoke and like Jake lit it from the fire. Little Jakie, not yet old enough to smoke, sat there staring into the fire, content to be with the men. The boy clearly felt that he had grown up somewhat and was on the verge of becoming a man himself.

'You bed down with your family in the wagon,' Arkansas said, addressing Jake. 'Rest that ankle because we've got some hard riding come dawn. I'll bed down out here and keep watch.'

'I'll take a watch,' Jake said.

'No,' Arkansas shook his head. 'Not tonight. You rest up and I'll keep an eye on things.' Arkansas stood up and arched his back and rolled his shoulders. 'In fact,' he added. 'I'm going to take a look around but don't worry. I'll be close by.'

Jake knew it was no good arguing with the man and he nodded and sat there with his son and watched Arkansas walk leisurely over to his horse. The man had done a full day's work and should have been plumb tuckered out but he moved with the agility of a mountain cat.

Arkansas mounted up and then tipped his hat to the man and boy before spurring his horse into a gallop.

'Where's he going?' Little Jakie asked.

'Like he said,' Jake said and smiled at his son. 'He'll be close by.'

'Lucy thinks he's Tumbleweed.'

'I know, son. I know.'

'He ain't though,' Little Jakie, being too old to believe such fancies said, and then added: 'Is he?'

Jake didn't answer the question immediately but remained silent, thoughtful for some time and when he did eventually answer it was with a smile.

'I think he's someone much like him, son. And that's all that matters.'

It was strange but with Arkansas now out of sight Jake could still sense his eyes upon them, feel him watching them, protecting them. He knew that with Arkansas Smith out there no one would be able to come within two miles of the camp without them knowing about it. And if those that came brought evil intent with them then the hot lead from Arkansas's guns would swiftly show them the error in their thinking.

They were safe; Jake didn't doubt that.

Just as safe as they would have been tucked up in bed at their new Kansas City home. Well maybe not quite that safe, they still had the elements to contend with and a storm felt imminent, but they were certainly safe from another surprise attack from the bandits.

From the diary of Ellie-May Preston

The man we called Arkansas Smith set Jake's ankle properly and once more Jake uttered nary a groan though he did fall unconscious for a while afterwards. It is strange but it now feels natural to have Arkansas with us. It is as if he is part of the family and not the stranger he truly is.

There is the feeling of a storm in the air, which worries Jake mightily though he does not share his concerns, else he worry us. I however know him so well and I can read his concerns in his eyes. His lips may remain silent but I can hear what he is thinking. It is one of the things that make us so strong together, that we have some kind of bond that almost seems supernatural.

I now feel easier about the journey still ahead of us. Maybe I too, like Lucy, am starting to believe that this man Arkansas Smith is the answer to our prayers. He might very well be. It is strange how Jake told us all the legends of the man called Tumbleweed and then this Arkansas Smith turns up to fill the role of this phantom of the imagination. Of course I am not suggesting for a moment that Arkansas is Tumbleweed – I leave such fancies to Lucy and her father – but he has certainly provided us with the protection of the fancy in the fairy-tale.

And what a tale of fancy it is for Jake told it all to us just as his father and his father before told it. It is indeed a wild fancy but one that provides comfort for those who chose to believe.

No one knew Tumbleweed's real name but the legend stated that he had been born in 1730 and was among the first whites to ever reach the land we now call America. It also told that he and his mother were the only survivors of a shipwreck, washed ashore like driftwood. And when the woman had ventured inland seeking sustenance for her and the child she had developed a fever and fallen down dead. Her infant child, then no more than six months old, was found by a pack of wolves and taken off by them, where they raised him as one of their own. As the baby became a boy and then a man he had learned the way of the wolf and knew how to survive in the most inhospitable of lands. But the man, still with no name, knew that he was different from the wolves, which were his only family. He was said to have left his wolf pack and started wandering the wilds, carving out the trail they had named Tumbleweed. He was said to have been given the name by an Indian tribe who felt he had restless feet that always caused him to wander. He would never stay in one place too long, and, like a tumbleweed blown on the wind, he would always be on the move.

It was said that he could speak many languages; both those of men and animals, and many tales were told of his incredible feats. It was said that he had once rode a whirlwind tornado as if it were a bronco and would use rattlesnakes as lassos. He was said to have saved a wise medicine man from sure death by holding a conversation with the grizzly bear that was all set to eat the wise old

85

Indian. The medicine man had possessed great power and as a gift to Tumbleweed he had gifted eternal life so that the man could forever protect those that travelled the hills he so loved.

As the years went by the man called Tumbleweed had continued to roam the hills, carving out the trail that now held his name. It was said that those who travelled the trail, as long as their hearts held no evil intent, would benefit from the protection of Tumbleweed. They would need fear man nor beast for Tumbleweed, always unseen, would never be too far away as he watched over them.

Jake claims there is some truth in the folklore, but I'm afraid that I am much more pragmatic than my darling husband, and have no time for such fancies. Folklore – fake lore would be a better word.

THIRTEEN

The storm broke just after the dawn and cut short their breakfast.

It had been brewing for days but when it did come, riled up into a fury, it was sudden, seemingly without warning. One moment the sky was slightly overcast and then in a blink of an eye it was raining with a ferocity that raped the ground, penetrating with enough force to spit up little clouds of dirt. Lightning shot through the sky like luminous serpents, lighting up the surroundings.

'We've got to move,' Arkansas had to shout to be heard over the raging wind that lifted his hat from his head and sent it spinning through the air. Thankfully the hat became caught up in the tall grasses maybe twenty feet away. Arkansas ran and retrieved it, pushed it down further onto his head and tied it with his bandana, knotting the now shabby but once gay material beneath his chin.

'It's going to get worse,' Jake shouted and stumbled as he tried to pull his own horse under control.

Damn and blast the broken ankle. He was useless.

'You drive the wagon,' Arkansas yelled. 'Hitch your horse behind. I'll lead and everyone else gets inside the wagon. It's blowing mighty fierce now. Let's keep moving for as long as we can, cover as much ground as possible.' The rain hammered into his face, drowning out most of his words.

Jake got the general gist though and he tied his horse next to the mule behind the wagon. Both beasts were skittish and shook their heads against the relentless pelt of the rain. Jake bowed his own head and, using the side of the wagon box to support himself, he slid himself across to the front and then climbed up onto the box. He popped his head through the canvas and smiled at his wife and children before turning back to the matter at hand.

'We're ready,' he shouted.

'Then let's move,' Arkansas yelled and spurred his horse into action. The creature bowed its own head and started to trudge forward, the ground beneath its hoofs now a mud bath.

Jake pulled his hat down low to shield his eyes from the worst of the rain and he yanked his bandana up over the lower half of his face. He guessed he must look like a bandit, not that anyone would be able to see him through this rain that was coming down so thick and fast it was like riding through a waterfall.

If only the storm had held off until they had reached the Great Forest, which was still, even in the best of conditions, a good day's ride away but at the moment it might as well have been a million miles distant.

Soon, Jake feared, if the rain persisted, they would have to stop as the wheels of the wagon refused to move and sank into the ground. Already the thick mud was sticking to the wheels and made the wagon all the more ponderous for the horses to pull. And the wind was hitting the canvas of the wagon, which made steering difficult, as it acted as a sail, trapping the wind.

The pace had become that of a slow crawl and Jake had to squint his eyes against the relentless driving rain. Arkansas couldn't have been more than ten feet ahead of them, riding carefully, ensuring the wagon wasn't driven into a newly formed hazard, and yet Jake couldn't even see him though the storm.

Thunder sounded in the distance. Impossibly loud, it echoed and seemed to shake the very ground. A few seconds of deathly silence followed before the thunder sounded again, even louder this time, and then a sheet of lightning brightened up the cobalt sky and momentarily gave the world a brilliant glow.

Inside the wagon, Ellie-May was reading to the girls and she had to raise her voice over the deafening roar of the rain hitting the canvas. Little Jakie was sat just inside the wagon doorway, watching his father's back through the slit, wondering if he should offer to take a turn at driving. He was sure he would be able to handle the team and he knew his father was suffering with his ankle. Driving the wagon was easy enough at the best of times, but in this storm it became a ponderous weight and the wind resistance caused by the canvas meant that every inch of ground they covered was something of a minor miracle.

Suddenly the wagon lurched to the side and then movement stopped all together. Little Jakie went through the doorway and looked at his father.

'What's happened?' he asked.

'Darn wheel's stuck,' Jake said. 'We become bogged down.' He shouted to get Arkansas's attention and carefully lowered himself down to the ground. He turned back to his son. 'Tell your ma to stay inside with your sisters. We'll have this sorted out in no time.'

Arkansas turned his horse and sped back to the wagon. He dismounted and slapped the rump of his horse, and the creature promptly moved behind the wagon, gaining some shelter.

'She's stuck fast,' Jake said. The front wheels were almost completely submerged into the sodden ground.

'We'll have to remove the canvas,' Arkansas said.

'Remove the canvas?' Jake couldn't figure out the reasoning behind the bizarre request.

'Ride into the storm barrel-headed. There'll be less resistance to the wind that way and it should be easier for the horses to pull. We could stop here but the closer we can get to the forest the better. At least we'll get some cover from the storm if we make the valley.'

Jake nodded. 'Everyone's gonna' get mighty wet.'

'Can't help that,' Arkansas said, having to shout against the roaring wind that threatened to take his breath away.

'Then let's do it,' Jake said and turned back to the wagon, telling his family what they were going to do. They would be able to lay down in the wagon box and use the canvas as an oversized blanket, which would keep the worst of the rain off. It wasn't perfect and would leave them exposed to the wind but there was no other way. With the canvas removed, the wagon wouldn't be such a wind trap.

Arkansas started on the canvas ties while Jake climbed from the wagon and started pulling at the canvas. Between them the two men removed the canvas from the wagon framing and then Ellie-May and the girls wrapped it around themselves as well as covering the perishable provisions. Little Jakie insisted on sitting up front with his father and no one saw fit to argue.

'Go forward slowly,' Arkansas said. 'The wheel should work itself free of the mud.'

Jake did so and after a slight protest the wagon worked itself free.

'It's done,' he shouted.

'Let's ride on,' Arkansas said, smiling at the sight of the three heads poking out from beneath the canvas cover.

'Ride on,' Jake agreed.

The rain was now coming down harder than ever and the wind had also picked up. They would

91

perhaps be able to cover a few more miles before they were forced to stop and sit out the storm. That would be it though, a few miles at the most and the thought that the storm could continue throughout the day and into the night was worrying. The horses were skittish and it was clear the force of the rain was causing them problems. Only the hardy old mule behind the wagon didn't seem to mind and it raised its snout into the air, as if taking in the rain through its nose.

'Come on you beasts,' Jake said, flicking the reins and starting the team off, pulling the wagon forward once more. There was some resistance and for a moment it didn't seem as if they would move, but then with a squelching sound the wheels once again came free of the ground, which now had the consistency of quicksand, and once more they were on the move.

'There she goes,' Arkansas yelled and kicked his horse forward again. The sorrel, although bothered by the storm, answered to the command immediately and trotted forward.

'Storm,' Jake yelled to the heavens. 'Why, ain't nothing but a summer's shower. Take more than this to beat us.'

His yells were answered by a spit of lightning and a roar of thunder.

Progress though was slow, any slower and it would have been a standstill but nevertheless they continued onwards. Arkansas kept his head down into his chest, yet still the rain hit his face with a stinging force. Jake and his son did likewise and all of them must have felt that facing a band of bloodthirsty outlaws would have been simplicity in comparison to this attack from nature itself.

Nevertheless they did what they had to do and continued onwards, each yard covered by the wagon was a backbreaking toil, and the wind was so strong that even breathing became a difficulty.

To stop though was not an option.

FOURTEEN

Brady cursed but the blasphemy was carried off by the raging wind and no one heard. They needed to find shelter and rest out the storm. Their horses were tiring quickly and to continue was too dangerous to contemplate. They couldn't see more than a few inches in front of them and there were many hazards to avoid as they travelled through the hills trying to get ahead of Arkansas Smith and the sodbusters.

Trouble was at the moment they were exposed to the elements and had no choice but to continue onwards until they found somewhere to shelter.

They would have to find somewhere very soon. The rain was intense and had soaked each of them through to the skin, and Brady knew that rain such as this would get to the gunpowder in their ammunition, rendering their weapons useless. That was not something the bandit wanted to contemplate.

Not with Arkansas Smith somewhere ahead of them and the posse behind.

Brady thought for a moment of Kicking Horse.

The Indian had still to return to them and he wasn't quite sure how he felt about that. On one hand it could mean that the posse were so far behind that the Indian was still some distance away and would take his time returning, or on the other hand it could mean the posse had gotten to the Indian and were at this moment riding towards them. There was no way of knowing for sure how far away or how close to them the posse was.

Damn the weather, Brady dug his spurs harder into his horse. The beast was stumbling, digging its feet into the ground and didn't want to continue. Brady turned in his saddle to look at his men behind him but the rain lashed into his face and he had to look away, bowing his head. His hat felt heavy as if there were a gallon of water collecting in its rim. The water spilled over the rim and onto his face, running down over his eyes and tasting warm on his lips.

Blade brought his horse up level with Brady's and looked at him with squinted eyes. 'Mile or two ahead,' he said. 'There's a worked out silver mine. We can get out of this darned rain.'

Brady nodded and shouted, 'You know it?'

'Yeah.'

'Then take over,' Brady said and pulled his horse back, allowing Blade to take the lead. 'Get us out of this damn rain.'

FIFTEEN

Kicking Horse looked at the five men, all that remained of the once dozen-strong posse, and bowed his head in shame. He was a full-blooded Cherokee and yet he had allowed himself to be captured so easily, rode straight into the five guns.

'What do we do with him?' Dan Kane asked. 'If we're going on ahead we can't take him with us and leaving him here ain't no option.'

Marshal Emery shook his head. 'I guess we've got no choice. He'll just have to come with us,' he said.

'There's a storm ahead of us,' Kane protested. 'We'll have enough to contend with without babysitting this Indian.' The sky above them was murky but up ahead they could see huge billowing rain clouds as lightning lit up the far horizon.

'And he's bound to try and warn his men when we get close to the varmints,' Bill Tillbrook put in. 'Way I see it if we're gonna' try and catch up with Brady then taking this damn Indian along is not a choice.'

'We could kill him here and now,' Dave Ashton

96

suggested and smiled at the Indian.

'That may be the wisest thing to do,' Max Tant added, glumly.

'We're riding under the colours of the law,' the marshal said. 'We ain't no lynch mob. We don't kill in cold blood.'

'Can't take him with us,' Kane insisted. 'Can't tie him up and leave him here. We may not return and that would be a slower death for him than killing him here and now. Killing him now would be a mercy. He's sure enough gonna' hang if we take him in.'

'We ain't killing him,' the marshal said, firmly.

Kicking Horse, hands bound securely behind his back and feet tied at the ankles, watched the exchange between the men without any display of emotion. He was, however, tensing his arm muscles, trying to pull his wrist free of the binding. If he could work his wrists free then he'd be able to work the rope down over his hands.

'We got no choice,' Tillbrook put in. 'Not if we're going on in any case. The way I see it the only way the Indian lives is if we turn back now and take him in. And they're just gonna' string him up then. Just as well get it over here and now.'

'We ain't killing him,' the marshal said again. 'And we ain't turning back.'

'Then what the hell are we going to do?' Dan Ashton asked.

The marshal lit a quirly and sat down on a large rock. He pulled the collars of his sheepskin jacket tighter around his neck and smoked while he

thought the situation through. The men were right –
taking the Indian on with them would pose too much
of a risk but all the same turning back was not really
an option. Arkansas Smith was out there alone, and
the Lord alone knew how far ahead he was. The
Indian was saying nothing and the marshal knew
there was no way to get anything from the red man.
Torture wouldn't loosen his tongue but that mattered none since the marshal didn't have the
stomach to torture any man, red or white.

'The way I see it,' the marshal said presently. 'Is
there's five of us, six if we include Smith but then
Brady's down in numbers, too. I'm not rightly sure
how many men he's got with him now but it can't be
more than a handful and this Indian makes it one
less.'

'So?' Dan Ashton prompted, not sure where this
was going.

'So,' the marshal said. 'I reckon I can spare one
man myself. One of us stays behind with the prisoner.
Set up a camp and waits for the rest of us to return.'

'That's plumb loco,' Bill Tillman said. 'What if we
don't return?'

'I figure we're maybe a day behind Smith, two at
the most. If we ain't back in five days,' the marshal
said, 'then whoever stays behinds simply rides off
with the prisoner. He can report the rest of us
missing on the chase when he gets into the nearest
law office.'

'That's a lot of trouble for an Indian,' Kane said.
The wind was picking up some and soon they would

be riding into a storm.

'He's a man,' the marshal looked Kane directly in the eye, steel in his stare. 'And he's my prisoner.'

'He ain't no white man. He's a red man. No better than a wild animal.'

'A man nonetheless,' the marshal insisted. He'd known a great many Indians in his time, and some of them had been the most noble men he'd ever had the pleasure to know, but all the same he didn't bother to correct Kane's ignorance.

'I sure as hell ain't staying behind with this Indian,' Kane spat into the dirt.

There were grumbles from the other men and although none of them actually said anything, it was abundantly clear they also didn't relish the idea of remaining with the Indian.

'You men are deputised,' the marshal said, firmly. 'You'll do as I say. We'll draw straws and the shortest stays behind.'

'I ain't doing it,' Kane insisted.

The marshal got to his feet with a groan. 'You'll do it if you draw short,' he said and went and pulled up a handful of the thick grass. He selected four pieces and dropped the rest to the ground. Then, after snapping each blade so they were all equal in length, he snapped one in half again.

'This is crazy,' Kane said but everyone ignored him and all eyes were trained on the marshal.

Kicking Horse stared raptly at what was going on and he hoped that it wasn't the man called Kane who drew the short straw. The Indian suspected the man would put a bullet in him as soon as the others were out of sight, and then claim that he had tried to escape. He continued to struggle with his bonds but he was secured tightly and expertly. These men certainly knew how to tie a knot and all of Kicking Horse's struggles had not even loosened his bounds in the slightest.

'You men ready?' the marshal asked. 'Form a straight line. Shortest piece of grass stays with the prisoner.'

The men lined up next to each other, even Kane joined the line but he continued to grumble until the marshal stood before them and held out his hand, the four blades of grass protruded from his fist.

Kane went first, snatching a blade of the grass and then sighing his relief when he found he had selected a long blade. He slapped a knee and did a delighted little jig that shook his hat from his head.

Kicking Horse nodded, relief in his eyes.

'Next,' the marshal prompted.

Bill Tillman took a blade and also drew a long blade. That left two blades and two men – a fifty/fifty chance.

'If you men don't return the poor bastard left behind's got a job on his hands. It's a six-day ride to the closest town,' Max Tant said and took a blade of grass. He immediately bowed his head when he noticed he had drawn short. 'Ain't never been lucky. That's why I don't gamble.'

'I still say we're better off killing the Indian,' Kane

said and kicked up the ground.

The marshal ignored him and spoke directly to Tant.

'We'll leave you enough supplies,' he said. 'And a little extra for the prisoner. You keep a rifle, a side arm and spare ammunition.'

'Don't see why we should share our food with this murderous son-of-a-bitch,' Kane grumbled again and gave Kicking Horse a look of pure hatred.

The marshal ignored him and continued to address Tant.

'As I say, give us five days and then ride out. I figure if we're not back then we ain't coming back.'

Tant nodded, defeated.

The marshal tapped Tant on the shoulder. 'We'll be back,' he said and then turned to the others. 'Get mounted. Let's get on with this.'

'Well I'll just sit here and kick up my heels until you do,' Tant said.

The marshal took a sack of coffee from his own saddle-bags and handed it to Tant. Next he went around each man's saddle-bags in turn and took a few slices of jerky and some dried biscuits from each.

'You may be able to catch some critter for fresh meat,' he said and handed the provisions to Tant.

'Or you can eat the Indian,' Kane said, laughing and climbed into his saddle. 'Don't know what he'll taste like but some of them squaws can be mighty tasty.'

Kicking Horse glared at Kane with pure hatred in his deep brown eyes. At last he could feel some give in the bindings at his wrist, and he knew that in a few more hours of struggling he would be able to break free.

'If you don't quit that talk,' the marshal said, glaring at Kane, 'I'll put a slug in you here and now. And give the prisoner your share of the food.'

Kane said nothing more.

SIXTEEN

Once again the wagon had become trapped in the thick mud, the wheels sinking down to the axle, and it was clear that they wouldn't be able to go no further. They were now only a couple of hours' drive away from the forest, and had entered the valley, but they had no option but stop here and wait out the storm.

In an hour or two it would be dark in any case.

Arkansas looked around them. He would have preferred to have gotten to the forest, but they had at least entered the valley that ran down towards the forest. It only offered them limited protection from the raging wind and torrential rain but he supposed that was some mercy. He dismounted and walked over to the wagon, bending to examine the wheels.

'We'll hitch our own horses to the team,' he yelled to Jake. 'Then we'll put the canvas back on and set up camp here for the night. I don't think the storm's gonna' last too much longer. It's weakened some- what in any case.'

'Amen to that,' Jake said and with some discomfort got down from the wagon. He slid his makeshift crutch from the box and limped over to Arkansas.

'She's stuck good,' he said.

Arkansas nodded. 'Get everyone off, lighten the load and I'm sure the horses will pull it free. If not we can lay the canvas down under the wheels, pull it out that way.'

'What's happening?' Ellie-May asked, her head emerging from the sodden canvas.

Jake looked at her and smiled. She looked almost childlike with her head emerging from the canvas, which lay across her and the children like an oversized blanket.

'Snug enough in there?' Jake asked, good humour in his tone.

'Are we stuck again?' she asked.

'We're bogged down good and proper,' Arkansas said.

'Afraid you're all gonna' have to join us in the rain,' Jake said, addressing his wife. 'We need to pull the wagon free and then we'll set camp. Sit and wait the storm out.'

Ellie-May looked up into the grey sky and then wrinkled her nose, but said: 'Can't say I'll be sorry to make camp.'

'Then let's get moving,' Arkansas said. 'Soon as we get the wagon free we'll put the canvas back on. Make things more comfortable for everyone.'

It took a little over thirty minutes to pull the wagon free of the sucking mud and get the canvas back over the wagon barrels. The wind had let up some but it still made it a major chore fixing the canvas to the wagon. Each and every one of them, children included, were soaked through to the skin by the time it was done and Arkansas and Jake stood out in the rain while the women and children changed into fresh clothes, though even their fresh clothing was damp. By then the rain had let up some and was now little more than a drizzle but the wind still blew.

Jake changed clothing himself and then gave Arkansas a fresh shirt and pants. Once that was done they all felt a little better and when the rain stopped completely Arkansas was able to use some of the chips they carried in the box under the wagon and get a small fire going. There wasn't much in the way of dry wood around but Arkansas managed to collect together a bunch of kindling, which he lay besides the fire to dry out some.

'We'll make the forest before noon tomorrow,' Arkansas said, while they watched Ellie-May prepare a warm meal. As far as Arkansas was aware, the woman only had some beans, flour and animal fat to work with but the aroma the food gave off was exhilarating. 'I'll stay with you folks until we get through the forest. Then you'll be safe and have the Arkansas River to lead you all the way into Dodge.'

'I appreciate everything you've done,' Jake said and massaged his injured ankle.

Arkansas nodded. 'Truth be told,' he said. 'I've enjoyed my time with you folks.'

'You must come visit us in Kansas City,' Jake said, the offer genuine. He didn't care squat for all the stories he'd heard about this man called Arkansas Smith. He considered himself a good judge of character and from what he could see Arkansas was a mighty fine man.

Arkansas smiled. 'I may take you up on that one day,' he said.

'You'll sure be welcome.'

'Thanks.'

Both men stared at the fire, lost in thought. Behind them the three children sat in the wagon doorway waiting for the food to be ready, the two girls concentrated on a picture book, Lucy's ever present Miss Sally sat next to them, while Little Jakie sat staring out into the darkness, watching the two men smoke.

If Arkansas was honest with himself, the short time he had spent with the family had left an indelible mark on him. Maybe it had made him re-evaluate his own life and question the worth of his existence.

He was a wandering man and knew it was unlikely he would ever lay down roots and have a family of his own. Even if he was so inclined, which was something he wasn't at all sure about, Justice O'Keefe and the politicians who controlled him would never let him go. He had a death sentence hanging over him and was only ever one task ahead of the rope.

O'Keefe called him a blunt tool, a trouble-shooter for the government, someone to carry out the dirty work no one else wanted to do. And it was those lawmakers and politicians that kept the warrant for his arrest inactive. If he ever lost his usefulness to them then he had no doubt that warrant would come into force. Of course, they had promised him that a full pardon would come one day, that he'd be able to walk away a free man and live his life whichever way he saw fit, but Arkansas doubted that. It was far more likely that one day he'd take a bullet during one of the jobs O'Keefe set him, and no one would shed a tear when Arkansas Smith fell, there would be no one to mourn the man. And no doubt many would say good riddance when he was finally dead. Death, Arkansas figured, was his only avenue of escape from the position in which he found himself.

He flicked the remains of his quirly onto the sodden ground and sighed. It would do him no good to think along these lines, but all the same he couldn't help but envy Jake Preston. The man knew where he was going, had clearly defined goals to strive for. He had a loving wife and children who would carry on his name and his bloodline. Perhaps to some he would appear commonplace, totally unremarkable, just a man no different than a thousand others, but sitting here now, watching Ellie-May prepare the food, Arkansas would have given anything to swap places with the man.

'We'll move out at first light,' Arkansas said and then made himself another quirly.

107

From the diary of Ellie-May Preston

I sense a great sadness in this Arkansas Smith. It's not as if he says anything; he doesn't really say much of anything. It's more in his eyes, as if the chill of loneliness resides deep inside him and is visible within those deep blue eyes. At times he seems quite cheery, but there is a solemnity within his nature that he just can't hide.

He's travelled with us for a few days now and yet we know no more about him that when we first met. Indeed what we do know comes from the legends and stories told of him. For the name Arkansas Smith is well known in the West. If one believed everything that is said about him he would be a bloodthirsty killer, an Indian fighter, a lawman, and a violator of women, a government assassin and a demon sent by the devil to do his evil work. For all of these things, and more, have been said of Arkansas Smith. Some say that he is the fastest draw there ever was and that he rode with the border rebels during the war, raping and looting while towns burnt around them. It seems to me that at one time or another he has been blamed for everything from the assassination of President Lincoln to the great floods that led Noah to escape in his ark.

I doubt if even a smidgen of these stories are true, though.

From what I can see of him he seems a good, if troubled man. And whilst he is secretive about his past and reluctant to talk about himself in any substantial way, I do not and cannot see him as a bad man. Lucy has especially taken to him and I see the kindness in his eyes when he speaks to her. Lucy too seems comfortable around him and only Little Jakie is a little guarded but then the boy thinks of himself as protector of the family and is wary of anyone who does not share his own blood. It is in his nature to be like this. His father is very much the same, though Jake seems to trust Arkansas fully and the two men get on greatly. I think this is largely because Jake knows Arkansas will protect us from any danger. With his broken ankle, Jake knows he would be next to useless in a real fight and needs Arkansas Smith to help us get through to Dodge. There Jake will be able to see a doctor and the rest of our journey will be through much less hazardous territory.

We have just come through a ferocious storm with winds and rain that I never thought would end. The rain has stopped now and as I write the children are asleep besides me while Jake and Arkansas are sat outside by the fire, sharing small talk while they drink coffee laced with a little whiskey. Only a trace of whiskey though for the bunch of cutthroats led by Sam Brady are still out there somewhere, and whilst the men seem more relaxed we must constantly remain vigilant.

In country such as this it could prove fatal to drop our guard for even a moment. Who knows what would come in on the whispering wind?

At night like this it seems so peaceful and the air so fresh now that the storm has passed. There is cleanness about everything, as if the storm has washed away the dust and grime of a hot summer. We are camped within a valley, only a few miles distant lies the Great Forest and although the men have said nothing to neither the children nor myself, I have overheard them talking. They seem of a mind that once we have crossed the forest we are out of any danger, but I know they fear an ambush within the confines of the forest. And the forest stretches for many miles, with each of those miles offering ample places for men to conceal themselves and lay in wait for us to come by. This is a big country and the perils faced are just as immense. One cannot afford to lose one's vigilance for even a second; each and every second is spent on constant alert.

I long to reach Kansas City and restart our lives, to worry about the mundane everyday things and not fear a killer may be lurking over our shoulder or a tribe of warring Indians waiting to attack us. And yet this has been a great adventure and I suspect that in time we will all look back on these days with a certain fondness.

SEVENTEEN

'Good thing the rain's ended,' Brady said, smirking at Blade. 'Ain't no shelter to be found there.'

Blade removed his hat and ran a hand through his thinning hair.

'Last time I was through this way the entrance was open. Landslide must have blocked it all up.'

'Or dynamite,' Brady said. The rocks above the old mine shaft certainly bore the scars of an explosion. 'Who knows? Don't really matter none in any case.'

'Why would anyone want to do a thing like that?' Blade asked but received no reply.

Brady looked around.

Even with the old mine entrance now concealed by the landslide, this was as good a place as any to rest up for a few hours. The pace during the storm had been slow, almost a crawl, and the old bandit felt that if they rested for just a few hours the horses would be fresh.

They could ride out before dawn and catch up with Smith and the sodbusters, who surely couldn't be too far ahead now. It would have been slow going with the wagon at the best of times and the storm would have stopped them almost completely. Brady guessed that they would be somewhere in the valley a few miles ahead, heading towards the forest that would eventually bring them out onto the plains that ran all the way down to the Arkansas River.

Soon, Brady thought. Very soon he would send Arkansas Smith straight to hell.

He dismounted, led his horse towards the cliff face and worked a kink out of his neck. Immediately weary, he sat down on a small rock and closed his eyes.

'We rest,' he said. 'Two hours. No More.' With that the old bandit slept. Sitting there upon the rock, his face resting in cupped hands, he slept as soundly as if he had been stretched out on a soft feather mattress.

With the exception of Blade, the rest of the men dismounted and, as if oblivious to the saturated ground beneath them, sat with their backs against the rock face. In almost one synchronized movement they each pulled the brim of their hats down over their faces and then were still.

Blade looked first at Brady and then at the other men. He shifted uneasily in his saddle and for a moment he considered pulling his gun and blasting Brady away while he slept. He was sure he was better qualified to lead this gang than Brady, who was getting old and soft, and no longer had the heart for banditry.

Something, however, stayed his hand. Perhaps it was the fear of not killing Brady with a single shot and having Brady make a fight of it with the rest of the men sticking by their leader. Blade wasn't really sure why he didn't fire and, other than the fact that it had nothing to do with loyalty to his leader, he was at a loss to understand what prevented him acting on his impulse. More than anything else he wanted to take over control of the gang and he knew the only way he would ever achieve leadership was with Brady dead and gone.

'I'm gonna' look on ahead,' he said and other than a mumbled reply from Tommy, no one seemed to have heard him.

He spurred his horse into a steady trot and continued along the trail. He wasn't sure how far he had travelled when he detected the aromas of wood smoke in the air, but he guessed it must have been several miles. He had been lost in thought as he rode and night had now fallen, the entire landscape covered by an inky blanket with little or no illumination from the moon, which glowed weakly through thick clouds. He had entered the valley that led towards the Great Forest and he pulled his horse to a stop, straining his ears to pick out any sounds.

Blade shivered.

There was a chill in the night air and his damp clothing made him feel the cold. He ignored his discomfort though and held his horse steady. There was no mistaking the sweet scent of burning wood and he peered in the darkness, looking for a flicker amongst the thick night, but there was nothing.

Cautiously he set his horse off at a slow pace, little more than a trot, and he sat alert in the saddle, ready to draw his guns at any moment. At one point he imagined he could see smoke, milky white, drifting against the far horizon but there was too much cloud cover to be sure.

The scent of fire though was stronger than ever and Blade was ready to spring into action at the first signs of danger.

He smirked, thinking that if he finished Smith off now, took him and the sodbusters out while Brady slept, then maybe he'd be able to take over leadership of the gang without having to put a bullet into Brady's brain. Though he'd do that anyway, but he would like to be in charge before he did, so that he could be sure the men would stand with him and not fight for their slain leader.

Brady was past his best and Blade knew that if he managed to get Smith and the sodbusters it would prove it. If he did this alone, did what Brady had failed to do even with all the men behind him, then those men would side with him. Surely they must for their leader had already lost many men, men who had ridden with them for years, fought, laughed and cried with them, men who had been their friends and comrades in arms.

It was then that Blade thought he heard something. He kept his horse perfectly still while he listened, holding his own breath as he strained his ears to pick up something. He couldn't be sure but for a split second he'd thought he'd heard the whinny of a mule somewhere in the distance.

'Come on,' he whispered to his horse and kicked his heels, setting the animal off into a canter.

Visibility was still poor. The storm was now well past but the thick clouds remained, filtering the weak glow of the moon. There was not even a star visible in a rheumy charcoal grey sky.

Blade rode at the same steady pace for some time before he spotted the unmistakable glow of the campfire in the distance.

He pulled the horse to a dead stop and smiled.

'Found them,' he whispered, blowing his fetid breath into the horse's face. He checked his six-guns and then the Winchester rifle. Finally, he felt the heft of his Bowie knife and then, satisfied, he set the horse off in a slow trot, wanting to get as close as he could to the camp before he was heard. With luck he could get close enough to take the men out before they even noticed him coming.

Blade grinned again as a wicked notion formed in his mind.

With the men dead he would be able to have some fun with the woman before killing her. The thought excited him and his eyes took on a steely glare as he rode on towards the ever-growing glow in the distance.

EIGHTEEN

Kicking Horse was all but free.

He had worked his wrists free, though for the moment he kept them behind his back as if still bound while he watched the white man by the campfire. The man was dozing and Kicking Horse knew that all he had to do was wait a little longer and then he would be able to remove the rest of the rope that bound him with ease. He sat back against the tree to which he was secured, a thick rope around his waist and then wrapped around the tree, and smiled.

With luck he would be able to escape into the night before the white man even stirred. Kicking Horse saw no reason to kill the white man. After all, he had treated him well enough. The Indian wished it had been the white man called Kane guarding him. It would have been a great pleasure to kill the one called Kane.

Dawn was no more than a few hours away and Kicking Horse knew that his best chance of escape was in spiriting himself away under the cover of darkness. He closed his own eyes but remained alert, listening to the white man's breathing. It was becoming rhythmic, deep, as he drifted further into true sleep.

When Kicking Horse next opened his eyes the white man was fast asleep and snoring like thunder. The Indian pulled his hands free from behind his back and massaged each wrist in turn.

The struggle to break free of the rope had grazed his wrists and the red rawness stung, but the Indian ignored the minor pain while he untied first his feet and then the rope around his waist. He had been in this seated position, bound to the tree for many hours, and he had to stand up slowly and allow the feeling to return to his legs before moving.

Kicking Horse stood there for many minutes, first wriggling the toes within his moccasins and then bending his feet, pushing himself up onto his toes. Finally, cramped muscles loosened up as the blood started flowing again, and the Indian moved forward on silent feet.

He cautiously reached for the Winchester next to the sleeping man and managed to grab it without disturbing the man.

Kicking Horse smiled.

This was good.

Next the Indian went down onto bended knees and reached across and carefully slid the Colt from the sleeping man's holster. At one point, with the gun only halfway out of leather, the sleeping man stirred and for one awful moment the Indian thought the man would wake and that he would have to kill him, but the man merely smacked his lips and went back to his snoring.

The white man was now unarmed and, satisfied that he no longer posed a danger, Kicking Horse went to the horses that were tethered to the stump of a dead tree. The Indian whispered to the horses and then untied them both. He climbed onto the back of his own horse and, holding the reins of the second horse, he let out a blood-chilling scream and sent his horse galloping away, pulling the second horse behind.

Tant came awake immediately, jumping up with a yelp, his hand going for his sidearm but finding only empty leather.

'Damn,' he said and looked for his rifle, only to find that this too had gone. The Indian had gone and taken all his weapons with him, leaving the man helpless and with no way of pursuit.

Tant reached into his pocket and pulled out a plug of chewing tobacco. He bit of a chunk and threw his hat onto the ground in frustration. He sat himself down by the fire and buried his face in his hands.

'Damn,' was all he said.

NINETEEN

Blade was close enough to take a shot.

He didn't want to risk it, though.

Not quite yet.

He had the advantage of his presence here being unknown, and it would be a shame to waste it.

He wouldn't take a shot until he was sure of his target, which meant getting a little closer still. He could clearly see the man they called Arkansas Smith sitting by the campfire, the wagon a few feet behind him. However, he was at an awkward angle and it was too tricky a shot from here. No one else was visible and Blade guessed that the others were inside the wagon. That was good for as soon as he had taken care of Smith the occupants of the wagon would provide a turkey shoot.

'Bang,' he whispered, his finger tensing on the trigger of his rifle but he didn't fire.

He needed to get closer.

He got up and silently walked back to his horse, which he had ground-tied a few yards away. He took up the reins and silently led the horse back the way they had come. He didn't mount the horse but led the creature for a good quarter of a mile before tethering it to a spindly-looking tree. The horse was now far enough away from the camp so that any sound it made would not be heard.

Then he made his way back towards the camp.

He reached his previous position in good time and was pleased to see that Smith was still sat in the same position, head bowed towards the fire. Blade crouched down behind a large rock and then, after checking Arkansas's position and seeing the man hadn't moved, he lay forward on his belly and slid along the ground, moving closer to the camp.

He was aware of the sound of his own breathing. It sounded impossibly loud to Blade, loud enough even to be heard by the man down by the campfire, but the man heard nothing and Blade soon reached a position where he felt he couldn't miss, there being less than thirty feet between him and his target, and from his elevated position he knew that he himself made a far too difficult target for any retaliation.

Only there wouldn't be no retaliation and Blade felt that he'd be able to pick them all off without a single shot being sent his way.

That was just the way he liked it.

He checked the workings on his Winchester, sending a slug into the chamber and slowly, very carefully, took aim. He watched the man in his sights and he guessed he must have been sleeping. The man hadn't moved for some time, his hat pulled down over his face and his coat all bunched up around him.

Blade smiled and aimed dead centre of the sleeping figure's hat. He increased the pressure on the trigger and fired.

'Stand up slowly and drop your guns,' the voice came from behind Blade.

Two things happened at once, confusing Blade. First, the hat responded from his shot by flying up into the air, revealing nothing beneath it, the coat sliding to the ground. And then that voice spoken from behind him and coming from where previously there had been no one.

It was all too much for the outlaw and his brain rebelled at the possibility of the man vanishing from the campfire and suddenly materialising behind him. No, it was all too fanciful for Blade to consider and he guessed that the damn Indian suspicions around Arkansas Smith had shaken him up some. It was Kicking Horse and Flightless Eagle with their stories that had rattled him. Men couldn't just vanish and reappear somewhere else. Smith must have been behind him for some time and somehow managed to place his hat and coat in that position. Maybe he'd done it when I led my horse away, Blade reasoned.

Weren't anything supernatural about Arkansas Smith.

He was just very slippery is all.

Blade turned his head over his shoulder and looked directly into the ice cold and fearless eyes of Arkansas Smith. The outlaw shivered and had to bite

121

his lip to bring himself under control.

'Stand up slowly,' Arkansas repeated.

Blade left the rifle on the ground and cursed as he climbed to his feet. He stood there, hands raised.

'Unbuckle your gun belt,' Smith ordered, the eye of a single Colt pointed at Blade's belly.

'You hoodwinked me,' Blade said.

Arkansas smiled and repeated: 'Unbuckle your gun belt,' this time he prodded his own gun forward as if the emphasize the command and added, 'You don't want to be gut shot.'

Blade agreed, indeed being gut shot had never been on his list of priorities; it was actually something to be avoided. Slowly he reached down and unbuckled his belt. He allowed it to fall free of his body and then put his hands back up. He heard movement behind him as the sodbusters investigated the commotion.

'Now turn around,' Arkansas said. 'Walk slowly towards the camp. I'll tell you when to stop and you'd better not be hard of hearing.'

'I had you,' Blade said, still stunned by the sudden reversal of the situation. 'I could have killed you.'

'You killed my hat,' Arkansas said. 'And that's all you're going to kill.'

Blade still had a gun, though. A small Derringer that he'd taken from the body of a suddenly deceased city gent several years back. The gun didn't have much stopping power but at close range, which was the only way to use the thing, it was devastating. The outlaw clung to the hope that with the gun he would be able to turns things his way.

'Just don't shoot,' Blade said.

'Walk.'

'Sure. Don't shoot.'

Blade walked on cautious feet towards the camp. He saw the other man, the one who led the sod-busters, being supported by the woman. The man had his left foot all bandaged up and he had a makeshift crutch beneath his arm. The woman cradled an oversized rifle, a Sharps, beneath her own arm and the three children, two girls and a boy stood behind their parents.

As he drew closer Blade noticed what it was that had supported Smith's hat and coat.

There was nothing supernatural about it, merely a curiously shaped branch protruded from the ground, a single sleeve of Smith's coat still attached to it. It was the oldest trick in the book and Blade, like a greenhorn fool, had fallen for it.

'I'll be dammed,' Blade said.

'Mind your stinking mouth,' the cold metal of a six-gun prodded him in the back.

Blade continue to walk forward and by the time Arkansas ordered him to stop, he was close enough to the fire to feel its heat against his pants leg.

'Now sit down,' Arkansas ordered. 'Bend your knees and go down slowly. Keep your hands where I can see them.'

It was a difficult manoeuvre but Blade managed to get down onto his rump while mostly keeping his hands raised. He did drop his hands at one point,

123

when he fell backwards. He quickly reached for the sky again just as soon as he had righted himself.

'Keep them up,' Smith said and purposely walked around Blade until he was standing directly in front of him, positioned between the outlaw and the sod-busters.

'You're the one called Blade?' Arkansas asked.

'Yeah,' Blade nodded, seemingly pleased that Arkansas had recognized him. All the newspapers ever seemed to write about was Brady, Brady and more Brady, while the men of his gang remained largely anonymous.

'There's a good likeness on your papers,' Smith said. 'Only in the flesh you look a bit more like a weasel.'

'You came around behind me,' Blade said. 'I had you dead in my sights. Damn dirty trick.'

'You made enough noise,' Arkansas said. 'And I won't tell you again about your language.'

Blade frowned. He momentarily considered going for his concealed gun, taking Smith by surprise and sending a Derringer slug into that mocking face, but he decided against it. He needed to wait, bide his time and catch the other man off guard. Just as he had been caught off guard when Smith had sneaked up behind him.

'I do apologize,' Blade said and turned his head to give the man, woman and children a smile full of teeth like tombstones.

Dawn had now broken and weak light was filtering through the angry-looking sky.

Ellie-May quickly ushered the children over to the wagon and Jake, using his crutch, made his way over to stand by Arkansas. Blade noticed that the man was unarmed and now that the women and children had climbed up into the wagon, taking the rifle with them, it left only the one gun on the outlaw. The problem was, Blade reasoned, that gun was in the hands of Arkansas Smith and he had another in the tied-down holster.

'Where's Brady?' Arkansas asked.

Blade looked at him but said nothing.

Arkansas glanced around as if to ensure himself that the women and children were out of sight, and then lifted a foot and brought it down into Blade's groin, causing the outlaw to squeal as he was sent flailing backwards.

'I won't ask again,' Arkansas said and approached the now cowering outlaw.

Blade tasted blood on his tongue and the back of his hand came up red when he wiped it across his nose.

'I'm bleeding,' he pleaded.

'You'll bleed a lot more if you don't tell me what I want to know,' Arkansas said. He bent at his knees and crouching, pointed the Colt into Blade's terrified face. 'Where's Brady?'

It was then that all hell broke loose.

TWENTY

The posse was still someways back but they had all heard the gunshots. It sounded to them as if there was a full-scale battle going on a few miles ahead.

Arkansas Smith, though, knew none of this; indeed he had all but forgotten the long-errant posse, and although it would have been good news to him, it is doubtful that he would have had time to consider the fact that help was on the way.

Dust blew up at Arkansas's feet and he dove for the ground, seeing the flash of rifle fire from the banking where Blade had concealed himself. That answered his question as to Brady's whereabouts, and as he hit the ground he saw one of Blade's hands vanish into a boot and then return toting a small Derringer.

Arkansas swung his Colt and fired before the outlaw had a chance to use the small gun and Blade's expression of agony was obscured by a thick spray of crimson as his head swung back in reaction to his throat suddenly being torn apart by hot lead.

Arkansas rolled and positioned himself behind Blade. The outlaw was still alive but only just as blood gurgled from his open mouth as he spluttered his last few breaths. Arkansas cast a glance over his shoulder and saw both Jake and Little Jakie lying in the doorway of the wagon. They both held rifles but given the amount of natural cover the outlaws had they could find nothing to shoot at.

'Get everyone out of the wagon,' Arkansas shouted. 'It'll be safer to get them down behind it.'

A rapid volley of fire was sent down from the banking and Arkansas buried his face in the ground as bullets tore up the earth around him. Blade's body jittered as several wide shots punched into his dead flesh.

For a moment there was silence save for the echo of gunfire, which seemed to hang tangibly in the air.

Arkansas guessed there were at least five guns concealed upon the banking. It didn't seem that things could get any worse since the outlaws were in an elevated position and only had to pull back from the edge of the banking to render themselves invisible.

'Everyone OK?' Arkansas yelled back over his shoulder.

'We're fine,' Jake shouted back. 'They won't be able to hit us here.'

Arkansas heard Lucy cry that she had left Miss Sally in the wagon but her mother quickly comforted the young girl, and her sobs died away. The wind suddenly picked up some and Arkansas gave a silent prayer to whatever deities it is that gunmen hold dear, pleading that the rains would hold off. The situation was bad enough without the rain returning and making it worse.

'Brady,' Arkansas shouted and then when no answer was forthcoming: 'Brady, why don't you answer me?'

For several long moments there was silence but then Brady's voice rang out. 'You trying to guess positions?'

'Don't seem any point,' Arkansas yelled back, his eyes scanning the banking for any movement but he saw nothing. 'You've got yourself well hidden but then so have we. You or your men can't take a shot without exposing yourselves, just as we can't.'

'We can wait,' Brady answered.

'What we've got here is what's called a Mexican standoff.'

'You're in the weaker position,' Brady shouted back. 'Plus I've got more guns. This isn't any standoff. All I've got to do is bide my time and then pick you off at my leisure.'

'What makes you think you've got time?' Arkansas shouted back.

From the sound of Brady's voice Arkansas felt he had more or less pinpointed his position. For a moment he considered making a run for the banking, taking a chance that the surprise movement would throw the bandits into disarray, that he would prove too slippery a target, and allow him to pick a couple of them off before they got him. However, he had used that tactic on Brady before and then he had

had a fully armed posse with him. It was doubtful Brady would be taken by surprise again and so instead Arkansas spoke over his shoulder, keeping his voice too low to travel to Brady and his men.

'You keep your eyes peeled,' he said. 'Take a shot at the first chance.'

'I'm ready,' Jake answered. 'With Ellie-May and Little Jakie passing me a fresh rifle and then reloading I reckon I can do the shooting of five men.'

'I'm gonna have to make a run for the banking,' Arkansas said and then took several deep breaths while he readied himself to suddenly spring forth. It seemed the only way to break the stalemate.

Before Arkansas could move though, Brady and his men suddenly opened fire and he was forced to once more eat dirt. Slugs bounced off the ground around him, Blade's body twitched as even more bullets tore into him. And several shots tore holes in the wagon canvas.

Silence fell once more and Arkansas turned around to check on the others. He was relieved to see Jake giving him the thumbs up, signifying that no one had been hurt. Lucy's sobs could still be heard but they were softer, while the other two children remained silent.

That was good and so far the children were holding up well under this terror.

The last thing any of them needed now was a hysterical child.

'Next time we will kill you,' Brady shouted.

'You've got to find a target first,' Arkansas shouted

back. He looked around them and saw a patch of rocks and gorse about twenty feet behind the wagon. That would provide them with better cover but the problem was crossing the ground to the rocks. They would be completely exposed while doing so and Arkansas knew that Brady would be quick to take advantage of such an opening.

He slid across the ground, heading towards the wagon, and was relieved to reach it without further gunfire. He pulled himself those last few feet and lay on the ground next to Jake.

'I figure there's five of them,' Arkansas said. 'Blade's dead, so that should leave six of them but I can only hear five guns. Maybe they've lost another man along the trail somewheres. I know I hit one of them earlier and maybe he bled out,' Arkansas said, remembering the trail of blood that night when he had first met the Preston family.

How many days ago was that now?

Arkansas wasn't really sure but he knew it felt like months.

Jake nodded his head in agreement.

'You see those rocks?' Arkansas pointed and Jake nodded his head. 'I figure we'll get better cover there. You think you can get over there fast if I provide cover fire.'

'Sure thing. Even with my busted ankle.' Jake said. 'But I'll stay with you. Let Ellie-May and the children get over there first.'

Arkansas looked at Jake and was about to protest when he had a change of mind and nodded his head.

The injured ankle would slow Jake down and Arkansas guessed it would be quicker to drag him over once the women and children were already behind cover.

'With us both firing we can cover double the distance,' Jake said, logically. 'Let one of those varmints raise their head and I'll blast it off.'

Arkansas smiled and when he next spoke it was directly to Ellie-May.

'When we say,' he said, 'You grab the children and get behind those rocks over there. You don't look back, whatever you hear until you get to those rocks.'

Ellie-May looked towards her husband for guidance.

'Mind what he says,' Jake said.

'I'll stay with you,' Little Jakie said.

'No,' Arkansas said, firmly. 'You go with your mother and sisters.'

'But—' the boy protested. He didn't get to finish before he was cut off by his father.

'Mind what he says,' Jake snapped.

'Miss Sally,' Lucy said and tried to break free of her mother's embrace.' I can't leave Miss Sally.'

'Hush now,' Jake said. 'We'll get your doll later.'

'On the count of three,' Arkansas addressed Ellie-May directly, 'You grab those children and run for cover.' He wiped a cold sweat from his forehead and shivered as the wind intensified further and then spoke to Jake. 'Fire on three and keep firing.'

Jake nodded and then smiled at his wife and children. 'Run like the wind,' he said.

Lucy gave a token protest about her doll but the rest of them merely nodded, their expressions firm, resolute. They understood what had to be done.

'One,' Arkansas said and took one of the rifles from Jake.

'Two,' he aimed at the banking edge and sent a slug into the chamber.

'Three,' he yelled and pulled the trigger and then reworked the breech and firing again, repeating the motion until he needed to reload but before he did so he set off several shots with his Colt. Jake did likewise. His Winchester was quicker than the Sharps rifle Arkansas was using and he kept the bandits' heads down while his family ran for and reached the relative safety the rocks provided.

Their fire was returned and both Jake and Arkansas had to chew dirt until the hail of lead abated.

'You OK?' Arkansas shouted.

'I'm fine and dandy,'

'They made it?'

Jake glanced over his shoulders and smiled. His family were now safely out of sight.

'They did,'

'Good,' Arkansas said and then shouted to Brady. 'We could keep this up all day. First we fire and then you fire. Seems like an awful waste of good lead.'

'We have much to waste,' Brady shouted back and several of his men laughed.

Arkansas figured he knew more or less where Brady and a couple of his men were positioned but the problem was, he was not sure how many men Brady had up there.

He was guessing around five, but it wasn't something he was willing to bet his life on.

It was very much indeed a Mexican standoff. The current situation could continue all day. Arkansas didn't think Brady would risk any kind of move before nightfall but there was no telling what sneaky move the bandit would try once it was dark. For the moment they were safe but given the current overcast sky it could darken pretty early, by mid-afternoon even.

'We've got to get out of here,' Arkansas kept his voice low, for Jake's ears only.

'What do you have in mind?' Jake shifted to work a cramp out of his leg. His ankle must have been smarting right dandy but he showed no sign of the pain he must have been experiencing.

'Don't rightly know,' Arkansas admitted and once again took a look at the immediate surroundings. Brady's gang were upon the banking directly left, it rose at a slope maybe twenty feet before levelling out at the top. Ahead of them was little cover between here and the entrance to the vast forestlands but that was still some miles off. The rocks Ellie-May and the children hid behind offered the only real cover, but even there Brady's guns pinned them down. There seemed no way of moving without exposing themselves to almost certain death.

'Beats me,' Arkansas said. He figured the only chance they had was if he tried to rush the banking, get to Brady before he was picked off. That was risky, though. Perhaps too risky.

'Murdering varmints,' Jake spat in frustration. The wind continued to intensify and the canvas of the wagon fluttered about like a sail in a storm.

'Don't much like the feel of this wind,' Arkansas wiped a bead of sweat from his brow. The air was growing humid again.

'Wind, rain, bandits,' Jake smiled. 'We got them all.'

'Sure got the wind and bandits,' Arkansas agreed.

For a moment there was silence between the men but then Jake prompted, 'So what do we do?'

'Guess we play the waiting game,' Arkansas said.

'You still thinking of rushing them?'

'Maybe. I don't rightly know.'

'It'd be risky, maybe too risky.'

'I know, but it don't look like we have many more options.'

'Damn,' Jake said, obviously in full agreement with Arkansas's appraisal of the situation. The longer they waited though, the more dangerous it would become. And how long would it be before one of the children lost their nerve and popped up from concealment.

'I don't like it,' Jake said. 'Waiting don't do no side any good.'

'I agree with you there,' Arkansas checked each of his Colts in turn, spinning the chambers and then returning the weapons to their holster.

'So what do we do?'

'Guess we just wait awhile,' Arkansas said. 'Work

on their nerves some before making a move.'

'Sure is working on my nerves,' Jake said and checked his own rifle. There was no read need but it gave him something to do.'

It was then that the situation suddenly and dramatically changed.

TWENTY-ONE

Gunfire sounded in the distance as a group of riders suddenly appeared on the horizon.

'Looks like your posse's finally caught up,' Jake said and had to shout when he noticed both his wife and son had broken cover to see what was going on.

They quickly scampered back behind the rocks though when they saw Jake's expression.

'Look at that,' Arkansas said, his mouth hanging open.

Arkansas should have been jumping for joy at the sight of his posse, which effectively placed Brady and his men in the middle of a deadly crossfire. Likely he would have been, was it not for the sight that greeted him.

A sight that filled him with a feeling of dread that ran soul deep.

'She's a big one,' Jake shouted to be heard over the raging wind.

'Too big,' Arkansas said and stared at the spectacular sight. He had all but forgotten Brady and the posse as he concentrated on the biggest twister tornado he had ever witnessed.

In the distance wolves, shaken up by the storm, driven half crazy by the tension they could feel in the air, howled out in rabid-sounding terror.

The tornado was sweeping across the valley floor, moving northwards on a direct course with them. Huge chunks of wet earth flew around in the tornado's funnel and Arkansas saw a small tree ripped from the ground, roots and all, to be sent smashing into the ground many feet away. Large rocks were lifted from the ground and then cast aside as the tornado carved up everything in its path.

'We've got to get to cover,' Arkansas shouted and, casting caution to the wind, he got to his feet and pulled Jake to his own feet. The posse had now grown closer and were exchanging fire with Brady's men but the gunshots faded away as everyone stared at the awesome sight nature was providing.

Arkansas and Jake reached the rocks behind which the others were sheltering with not a shot being sent in their direction. The tornado had grown closer still and both men could feel its pull as they threw themselves down onto the ground. The horses used to pull the wagon started to buck and the terrified creatures broke free of their restraints and ran off from the rapidly approaching swirling winds.

Arkansas watched as the tornado neared them. It was heading directly for the wagon but, as wide as it was, he felt it would miss them. The outer winds were hitting them hard now and Jake was holding his family bunched into him, as they felt the pull of the winds that surrounded the incredible-looking but extremely deadly tornado.

Arkansas noticed that the posse had dismounted and were now sheltering somewhere themselves. Neither Brady nor his men could be seen and, save for the roar of the tornado, everything seemed eerily silent.

'Hold onto each other,' Arkansas shouted and watched the tornado approach ever closer still. It was now almost close enough to touch and all he could do was stare at it in awe, marvelling at its sheer power. It was capable of a level of destruction that even the most murderous of men could not hope to match.

'Miss Sally,' Lucy suddenly screamed as she watched the rotating windstorm bear down on the wagon. She suddenly broke free of her mother's grasp and ran for the wagon, screaming for her cherished doll.

Arkansas got to his feet to go after her but was immediately thrown backwards by the winds. He landed painfully and saw Lucy disappear through the doorway of the wagon just as the tornado struck and lifted the wagon into the air as if it were nothing more than a child's toy. The mule, still tethered to the wagon, went with it, being swung around and around in the air until its reins snapped and it was thrown to the ground. Incredibly the beast got immediately to his feet and, although stunned, started pulling at the long grass with its powerful teeth.

Arkansas noticed Blade's body as it was picked up by the storm. It danced gruesomely in the swirling winds before it too was cast aside, coming down with a sickening thud against the rocks they hid behind. A dead hand reached over the rocks and Arkansas shivered as he pushed it back over and out of sight.

The wagon was thrown violently though the air, it spun around several times, the canvas fluttering like crazy. The barrels snapped under the force of the wind and the canvas was pulled tight, like flesh over the skeletal frame.

Again Arkansas tried to get to his feet but the wind hit him back down like a punch to the jaw.

'Lucy,' Ellie-May screamed and had to be held down by her husband to prevent her from trying to get to her daughter, who was somewhere inside the wagon that flew around them.

'Stay down,' Jake ordered, his heart feeling as if it had jumped up into the back of his throat as he watched the wagon fly around and around within the pulsating funnel of the tornado.

For a moment the wagon seemed to hang sus-pended in the air before crashing into the banking and breaking into pieces.

Then day became night as the storm moved across

the banking, mutilating the ground, as if following a set course. Planks of splintered wood, chunks of earth and stones flew through the air like the fire from a Gatling gun.

TWENTY-TWO

It left behind it a silence like the end of the world.

'Lucy,' Ellie-May said and tried to scramble to her feet but she was still held down by her husband.

Jake looked around and then his eyes landed on the wreckage that had been the wagon but there was no sign of his daughter.

'I'll take a look,' Arkansas said, reading their concern as clearly as words in a book.

Now that the tornado had passed, the air seemed perfectly still and the temperature had risen several more degrees. Arkansas got to his feet but he didn't move before Brady's voice sounded out.

'We've got the little girl,' the bandit shouted, as if in answer to Ellie-May's concerns. 'We ain't gonna hurt her just as long as everyone stays calm.'

Arkansas looked at Jake and had to hold his hands out to stop the man getting to his feet and trying to rush Brady's position. Ellie-May and the children looked frantic and it was clear to Arkansas that the woman was close to hysteria, which would be the worst thing that could happen at this particular time. They needed to remain calm. If they were to save the girl they needed to keep themselves under control and not provoke a shoot-out, for he had no doubt that Brady would kill the little girl with little regret if he was placed in such a position.

'What you got in mind?' Arkansas shouted. He didn't think Brady would shoot now, not with the posse one side of him and Arkansas the other. The old bandit was in a no-win situation and would be smart enough to know that holding the little girl was now his only chance of escape.

'We're going to ride past you,' Brady said. 'Take the girl with us. When we reach the forest we'll leave her there to wait for you. By the time you get there we'll be long gone.'

'No,' Jake said and once again tried to get to his feet but Arkansas pushed him back down and gave him a stern look.

'Take care of your family,' he said. 'I promise you I'll get Lucy back.'

Ellie-May started to cry and Jake held her to him, comforting her.

'Call your men off,' Brady shouted. 'I don't want to harm the child but one shot comes our way and she's dead.'

Arkansas walked closer to the banking, each step slow though purposeful. He held his arms limp at his side but he was ready to draw immediately if Brady sent any fire his way. Once he was only a few feet from the banking he looked for the posse and saw

142

Marshal Emery standing in the distance, a rifle at the ready in his hands. He had three other men with him, all that was left of the once-strong posse.

'Emery,' Arkansas shouted.

'I hear you.'

'Hold your fire. They've got a young child.'

'Understood,' Emery said and Arkansas noticed him talking to his men, obviously warning them off any heroics.

'You accept my terms?' Brady yelled down. The old bandit had now come out of concealment and stood at the banking edge, Lucy held in his strong arms with the ugly eye of a Colt pressed to her forehead.

The young girl didn't struggle at all and seemed calm, positively surreal, as she clutched Miss Sally in her arms.

'Don't look like we have a choice,' Arkansas answered. 'I'm warning you. Do not harm the girl.'

'The girl is safe,' Brady said. 'And if there's no tricks then she'll stay safe. You have my word. She'll be left safe and alive at the forest.'

'Looks like we got no option but to trust you.'

'Then we're coming down.'

Jake came over and, using his crutch for support, stood next to Arkansas. He looked at the remains of the wagon and shook his head. It was beyond repair. Not that it really mattered now. All that mattered was getting Lucy back unharmed.

'Stay calm,' Arkansas whispered. 'Whatever you do don't try and go to Lucy. Let them go by.'

Jake nodded, said nothing.

'Go back to your family,' Arkansas said. 'Keep them calm also. You may have to restrain your woman as soon as she sees her daughter's face.'

Jake didn't argue but immediately turned on his feet and limped back over to his wife and children. He sat himself down on a rock, dropped his rifle and hugged Ellie-May tightly.

'Let them go past,' he said, speaking to his wife and children. 'We'll get Lucy back. I promise you that.'

'Jake,' Ellie-May said, her words wrapped around her sobs. 'My little girl.'

'We'll get her,' Jake repeated.

And now Brady and his men were coming down the banking towards them. Brady was in the lead; Lucy sat on the saddle in front of him, held firm by one massive arm around her waist. In his other hand the bandit held a modified Sharps Big Fifty, the hammer cocked. They rode in single file with the remaining four members of his gang following behind. At the rear of the procession rode Flightless Eagle.

The Indian looked Arkansas directly in the eye.

There was the hint of great respect on Flightless Eagle's face.

'Nice of you to oblige,' Brady said as he drew level with Arkansas.

Arkansas had to fight back the strong urge to pull his gun and chance a shot at Brady, blow him out of the saddle and then get to the girl before anyone had a chance to react. He knew that if he did so it would

144

mean the end of Brady and his gang because Emery and the posse would immediately open fire also, but it was all too risky and he wouldn't gamble with Lucy's life. If Brady set that big old Sharps on her she would be blown into pieces tiny enough to float on the wind.

'I'll settle with you later,' was all Arkansas said.

Brady pulled his horse to a stop and looked down at Arkansas, a smile spread clean across his ugly face.

'There won't be a later my friend,' he replied and started his horse off. As he rode past the Preston family he smiled at them also, and tipped his hat to Ellie-May. 'Your child will be safe,' he said.

'Please don't hurt her,' Ellie-May stammered.

'You have my word,' Brady said as if he were the child's uncle taking her out for a ride rather than an outlaw holding her captive. Lucy, for her part, sat calmly in his arms and didn't even look at her mother, instead keeping her eyes on her doll. She seemed perfectly fine but was obviously suffering from some kind of shock after her ordeal. It tugged at Ellie-May's heart to see her little girl riding off with the bandit but she welled up all her strength and managed to stand steadfast, comforting her other children.

The posse, led by the marshal, was riding towards them and Brady cast an eye over his shoulder and saw the four riders approaching. He looked directly at Arkansas and darkness came over his eyes.

'They could make me jumpy,' he said. 'My finger might slip on the trigger.'

'They won't attack,' Arkansas said. 'They know the situation.' He turned and held up a hand to slow Emery down. The last thing he wanted was for Brady to get jumpy, not with him holding the girl.

'Then *adios*,' Brady said and started his horse off into a gallop, his men following behind.

TWENTY-THREE

'You stay with these people.' Arkansas said, addressing the marshal. 'You continue towards the forest at a steady pace. Just plod along as if you're out for a peaceful afternoon's ride.'

'And what are you going to do?'

'I'm going to get ahead of Brady,' Arkansas said. 'I'll surprise them when they enter the forest. As soon as I get the girl I'll let off two shots in succession, hold for ten seconds and then let off another. That'll be the signal for you to ride like the wind. It ends today.'

'That's all very well,' Dan Kane said and bit off a chunk of chewing tobacco. 'But how are you going to get in front of Brady's lot without them seeing you?'

'There,' Arkansas said, pointing to the banking. 'I'll ride up over the crest. Come at the forest from the south. I should be able to get there without Brady noticing me.'

Jake stood besides Arkansas and when he spoke it was directly to the man. He ignored the rest of the posse as if they were not present.

'Please,' was all he said.

Arkansas nodded.

'Trust me,' he said and whistled for his horse. The sorrel immediately appeared and galloped down the banking, where it had been grazing on the long grasses. It immediately came over to Arkansas and nudged its owner with its nose. Arkansas checked his saddle to see that it was still secure and, satisfied, he patted the horse and mounted up.

'Round up these folk's horses,' Arkansas said. 'Salvage what you can from the wagon and give it an hour before setting off. Keep riding at a steady pace and don't speed up until you get my signal.'

'An hour's an awful long time,' the marshal protested.

'Brady will be far enough away by then that if he looks back he won't see I'm missing,' Arkansas replied.

'Just how do you think you'll get my girl?' Jake asked. 'You're just one man.'

'Brady'll be true to his word,' Arkansas said. 'As soon as he leaves her at the forest I'll get to her and send the signal.'

'And if he isn't true to his word?' Ellie-May asked.

'Then I'll take her,' there was a strength in Arkansas's words and despite the situation no one doubted that he could do what he said.

Sarah broke free of her mother's grasp and calmly walked over to Arkansas. She stood beside his horse, patted the creature and looked up, staring directly into Arkansas's eyes.

'Save my sister Mr Tumbleweed,' she said. It was the first time she had addressed Arkansas as Tumbleweed, as if the faith her sister felt had somehow been transferred to her, but no one really noticed and no one said anything.

Arkansas smiled. 'She'll be eating dinner with you later,' he said and then cast a look towards Jake and the rest of his family, nodding to them. Then he kicked his horse off and sent the magnificent beast climbing the banking.

Arkansas went some distance before turning the horse and starting towards the forest. He had gone maybe a quarter of a mile when he heard the sound of a horse coming up fast behind him. There was a large patch of scrub to his left and he guided his horse into it and positioned himself out of sight while he waited for the rider to come into view.

Arkansas held one of his Colts at the ready while he waited for whoever it was. He wondered if Jake had followed him, but he was sure the marshal would have kept them all together. Still, he supposed, Jake was worried frantic about his daughter and he guessed that could be a powerful motivator. Maybe the man had broken away and the marshal and the remainder of the posse had been unable to stop him.

Arkansas didn't have to wait too long for the answer.

He saw an Indian; one of those who had ridden with Brady, come galloping down the trail towards him. The Indian was low in the saddle, his head almost level with that of his steed, as he concentrated on the landscape ahead.

Arkansas waited until the Indian was almost level with him and then suddenly spurred his own horse forward, causing the other horse to rear up and throw his rider.

Arkansas pointed his gun directly at the Indian.

Kicking Horse was momentarily stunned and it took a few moments for him to recover from his fall, but when he did he looked up at the man on horse-back and smiled.

'You are everywhere,' he said.

Arkansas grinned back. 'Well I'm here sure enough.'

The Indian was both unharmed and unarmed. He had been carrying a rifle but it was still in the saddle boot of his horse.

Arkansas set his own horse gently towards the Indian's horse and reached out and grabbed the creature's reins. He pulled it towards him and then reached over and slid the rifle out of its boot and placed it across his lap. He already had his Winchester in his own boot but the extra rifle may come in handy when he went up against Brady and his men.

'What are you going to do to me?' Kicking Horse asked.

'I'm setting you on foot,' Arkansas said. 'Either that or I kill you. It's your choice.'

'You take my horse?'

'Yep, that's pretty much the way it is.'

'You are going after Brady?' the Indian asked.

'I am,' Arkansas said. 'And I don't need you alerting him.' He cocked his Colt and squared it up right between the Indian's eyes. 'It's your choice,' he repeated.

'Go,' Kicking Horse said. 'I will sit here for some time and ponder things.'

'Ponder things?'

'Ponder the fact that I am growing old and too easy to surprise. Ponder on the fact that you are no ordinary man and I have no wish to fight you.'

Arkansas grinned. He knew very well what the Indians thought of him.

'Glad to hear it,' he said and immediately set his horse off into a gallop, dragging the Indian's mount behind him. He'd set it free after a few miles, when he was far enough away for him to reach Brady before the Indian had a chance of recovering the animal and catching up with him. Not that he had much to fear from the Indian, who was completely without arms, but he had spent enough time with Indians over the years to know it never did to underestimate their ingenuity.

Kicking Horse watched Arkansas until the man was just a speck in the distance.

'Bad medicine,' he said, and stood up and started walking in the opposite direction.

TWENTY-FOUR

Concealed, the sorrel tethered to a tree beside him, Arkansas watched as Brady approached the forest.

The bandit reached the tree line and then stopped dead, casting a glance over his shoulder at the party following him. To the bandit's eyes, Arkansas knew that they were visible only as tiny spots on the horizon. There was no way that Brady would be able to count them and realize that Arkansas was not with them.

'Come on,' Brady said to the girl, his voice was almost gentle, child-like. 'You wait here for your ma and pa.' He lowered the girl gently to the ground.

'You're letting her go?' Jim Carter asked.

'I said I would,' Brady looked at his men in turn, waiting for any of them to protest but no one did and so he turned his attention back to Lucy. 'You wait here,' he said, his words almost kind. 'Your folks will not be very long. You see over there?' Brady pointed towards the specks on the horizon.

They were so far distant they could have been specks of dust.

Lucy looked and nodded.

'Well that's your parents, girl. You just wait here for them and they'll be here before you know it.'

Lucy nodded again, clutching Miss Sally to her chest, and smiled at the bandit. Despite all she had been through she obviously bore no ill feeling towards Brady. She couldn't understand that he was bad, knew nothing of the desperate deeds and wrongs that had to be tallied for.

All the little girl knew was that the man had treated her kindly.

'Goodbye,' she said.

'Goodbye,' Brady said and ordered his men to follow him as he led the trail into forest, where daylight suddenly became dusk.

Arkansas watched all this without moving an inch. Nor did he move when Brady and his men passed him by. At one point they were less than twenty feet away and yet they saw nothing. He waited for them to get ahead some and then dismounted and led his horse to where Lucy sat cross-legged on the ground. He bent to her and smiled and then lifted her, placing her in the saddle of his sorrel.

She looked positively tiny on the back of the magnificent creature.

'Now hold on, Lucy. Old Red here's gonna take you back to your folks.' He then slapped the well-trained horse on the rump and it set off at a steady speed. It may sound absurd but the horse was seemingly aware of the need to keep the little girl on its back. The horse would take her straight to her parents, of that Arkansas had no doubt. He thought about firing his gun, sending the signal he'd promised, but decided against it. Lucy was safe and Arkansas figured keeping the element of surprise was of paramount importance if he was to catch up with Brady and his men.

He watched the horse head back along the valley and then turned and walked into the forest.

The forest was dense, there were trees upon trees and a man could move faster on foot than mounted. It was easier to negotiate the various obstacles on foot and it was not long before Arkansas saw Brady and his men as they weaved their mounts around one tree and then another.

Arkansas pulled a Colt and fired into the air.

'Stop and throw down your arms, he shouted.

Brady and his gang listened to the first part of the command but they took no heed of the second, and before they had even dismounted they returned fire. Arkansas ducked, feeling the hot air as a slug passed perilously close to his left shoulder. He fired quickly and saw Jim Carter blown sideways out of the saddle.

A sudden hail of lead answered as the oversized Sharps sounded and Arkansas dove for a thick spruce, bark spat up in his face as a huge slug tore into the wood. He fired again and this time he saw Tommy tumble backwards, clutching his stomach, trying to prevent his guts seeping out from between his fingers.

Arkansas saw the fat man they called Chuck aim a scattergun and he fired simultaneously with the roar of the gun. He saw Chuck thrown backwards as the top of his head exploded, but yelled in pain himself when several tiny balls of red hot lead from the scattergun embedded themselves in his right arm; his shooting arm.

Arkansas fell to the ground and moaned when the air was forced from him. His injured hand couldn't grip the Colt and it fell from his paralysed fingers. He noticed the Indian mount up and gallop off, Brady cursing him as he did so.

And then everything went hazy and for a moment Arkansas saw only blackness as he fought the urge to let go and allow the approaching blackness to take him.

'You dead yet?' Brady shouted from the tree he hid behind.

'Hardly,' Arkansas answered and struggled to his feet. He may have had only one working hand but he sure wasn't going to go down just yet. 'Show yourself, Brady,' he shouted and then he did indeed black out, his knees buckling beneath him as he fell to the ground.

For how long he had been unconscious Arkansas couldn't be sure, but he felt it was only seconds. Feeling had returned to his injured hand and the pain was immense. He looked up and saw Brady standing over him. The bandit pointed the ugly eye of he Sharps directly at his face.

'You keep coming,' Brady said. 'You keep coming until you are killed.' The bandit stepped on Arkansas's injured arm and worked his heel into the wound, sending a blizzard of sheer agony through Arkansas's entire nervous system.

Arkansas gritted his teeth against the pain, he wasn't going to allow himself to scream out and he most certainly wasn't going to pass out again. If this were it for him, if death was to come now at the hands of this cheap bandit, then he would face it head on.

'*Adios* Arkansas Smith,' Brady said and smiled. He took aim with the big old Sharps that looked like a cannon to Arkansas.

Such was the ringing in Arkansas's ears that he didn't hear the low growl of the wolf, nor was he sure what had happened when the creature, driven half mad by the tornado, ravenous at the scent of blood in the air, leapt at Brady, attaching its powerful jaw, filled with razor sharp teeth to the man's chest. The wolf had come from nowhere and the crazed creature was in a kill frenzy.

Brady was thrown backwards, the wolf tearing at his flesh. The animal's muzzle dripped with warm blood as it tore at the man. Brady shot but it was more a reflex action than an attempt at fighting back, for the wolf had already bitten deep into his throat, tearing bone deep, and he was already dead.

Arkansas stumbled to his feet and gazed at the horrific scene before him. The wolf had run off at the sound of the gunfire, and Arkansas looked on at Brady's mutilated body, blood dripping from the jagged tear in the man's throat.

From the diary of Ellie-May Preston

As I write it's been more than a year since we arrived in Kansas City but I remember it as if it were but a few moments ago. That ride across the valley towards the great forest was the longest I had ever endured and should ever hope to, but our hearts were lifted when we saw our beloved Lucy coming towards us on the back of that magnificent horse owned by Arkansas Smith. She seemed unconcerned and indeed unaware of what had happened. I scooped her into my arms and feeling that I would never let her go again, I cried tears of sheer joy.

There was no sign of Arkansas Smith when we reached the forest, nor did we ever see him again though we still hear stories of him from time to time. His horse also vanished. One moment it had been trotting along with the men from the posse and then next it had gone. Run off in search of its master.

The strange thing was that the grizzly sight that greeted us, besides the dead bodies of the outlaw gang was that of their leader. I did not look myself but I overheard Jake talking to the others. Apparently he had been torn apart and when the men had found him there had been a lone wolf standing on a banking, watching over the dead bandit.

157

The wolf had run off as soon as we approached.

We searched all over for Arkansas but there was no sign that he had ever been there. It was as if, like the mythical Tumbleweed, he had vanished into thin air or transformed himself into an animal of the forest, a wolf perhaps, and vanished into the wilderness.

After a while we had no option but to push onwards, the marshal and the posse would accompany us for the rest of our journey. Though even now during the dead of night, I think back to that strange time and I wonder, sometimes I wonder if Arkansas Smith had indeed been the man they called Tumbleweed. Though I know I am being foolish. I am being foolish. Aren't I?